Copyright © 2023 by Yolanda Sfetsos
Cover Art © 2023 by TruBorn Design
First published in 2023 by DarkLit Press

ISBN 978-1-998851-14-0 (Paperback)
ISBN 978-1-998851-13-3 (Ebook)

W0008042

PRAISE FOR
Suffer the Darkness

"Yolanda Sfetsos is such an incredible horror author with an amazingly distinctive voice. Her writing is sharp, terrifying, and unforgettable, and *Suffer the Darkness* is among her best work to date. This powerful tale will haunt your dreams and never let you go."

- Gwendolyn Kiste, Bram Stoker Award-winning author of *The Rust Maidens* and *Reluctant Immortals*

"In the brief space of this fast-paced novella, Yolanda Sfetsos manages to sweep her readers through heartache and the supernatural, stomach-turning body horror, haunting imagery, and an epic ending I didn't see coming."

- Laurel Hightower, author of *Crossroads* and *Below*

"As with every Sfetsos release, we get her deft prose and emotion-charged pacing. But with *Suffer the Darkness* we get that x10 as we barrel through a paranormal-folklore story sure to keep you up late at night!"

- Steve Stred, Splatterpunk-Nominated author of *Sacrament, Mastodon*, and *Churn the Soil*

"Swerving a rehash of the classic possession trope, in *Suffer the Darkness* Sfetsos creates horrors so imaginative and so vivid that you won't want to look, but will be powerless to turn away."

- Kev Harrison, author of *Below*.

"*Suffer the Darkness* is a unique tale of supernatural horror with a wildly clever twist. A brutal tale of supernatural horror on a whole new level."

- Sarah Jane Huntington, author of *Cabin Terror*

"Sfetsos weaves a dark tale steeped in folklore, possession and the power of a mother's love that will leave readers wanting more."

- S.H. Cooper, author of *Inheriting Her Ghosts*

BOOKS BY
Yolanda Sfetsos

SUFFER THE DARKNESS

Yolanda Sfetsos

DARKLIT
PRESS

CONTENT WARNING

The story that follows may contain graphic violence and gore.

Please go to the very back of the book for more detailed content warnings.

Beware of spoilers.

CONTENTS

"Love is composed of a single soul inhabiting two bodies."

– Aristotle

Eugene, always.

BEFORE

Thursday
July 10, 2014

6:33am

"Do you remember the verse about Czort?"

"Yeah..."

"Do you want to hear it?"

"Yes."

"If you venture into the woods alone,
he'll be waiting for you.
If you look deep into his eyes,
he'll come for you.
If you're brave enough to stay,
he'll never let you go."

"Do you want to hear the next verse?"

"I... didn't know... yes."

"Good girl."

"If you keep your eyes open,
you'll see the darkness.
If you stare into the void,
you'll fall into the darkness.
If you surrender your soul,
you'll suffer the darkness."

"Molly, do you feel the darkness?"

"Yes."

"Do you see yourself in the darkness?"

"Yeah..."

"Do you surrender?"

The darkness was so beautiful, how could she say no? "I do."

Blazing flames spilled from those intense eyes, spreading fast across his mighty bulk until she was engulfed by fire. She didn't feel any pain when her spirit was severed from her shell.

Her body was now replenished, had become something new.

A hollowed-out vessel ready for the taking.

As the horde flowed into her body, she welcomed them all.

DAY ONE

Tuesday
November 10, 2015

2:00pm

Kaelyn Roscoe rushed into St. Jude's hospital, leaving the cool wind in her wake as the automatic doors closed behind her. Her pulse was racing, but as soon as her eyes made contact with his and the tears threatened to make an appearance, she took a deep breath of the antiseptic air to maintain as much composure as she could.

"Where is she?" Her modest-heeled shoes squeaked over the tiles as she watched him step away from the wall and head toward her. She shouldn't be angry with him, none of this was his fault, but it was hard to be respectful considering the circumstances. Even if Roy had tried so hard to help, and had been with her through every minute of this nightmare.

Kae was upset because she wasn't at the office when he'd stopped by to tell her the news.

This wasn't the way she'd imagined things would turn out. After all the silent wishes and the endless hope during her bleakest hours, she'd imagined a multitude of scenarios about the one outcome she'd wanted the most. But she never thought she'd be busy showing a house to newlyweds who were maybe interested in buying a property in Thicket because this small town seemed like such a nice place.

She hadn't contradicted their excitement by telling them that the woods had stolen her daughter.

"Kae." Roy's brown eyes were shiny with concern and his hands were reaching for her. "The doctor will be here shortly to explain—"

"I've been waiting *so* long to see her again," she said. "I need to know where she is *now*." Kae was a nervous wreck and wanted desperately to see Molly. Her hands were shaking so much, she'd barely managed to drive straight.

"I know." He took her elbow and led her into the adjoining corridor, away from the prying eyes in the waiting room.

She didn't care who was there to witness this, but appreciated his attention to detail. It was one of the many things she loved about him. If not for this man, she wouldn't have made it through this ordeal.

The doctor arrived before the urge to throw her arms around him consumed her.

"Mrs. Roscoe?"

She cringed at the mention of a surname she should've changed years ago.

"Yes, I'm *Ms.* Kae Roscoe." She'd been divorced for a while but laziness, or the need to have the same surname as her children, kept her from changing back to her maiden name. Even if Ventura had always suited her better than Roscoe.

The middle-aged woman nodded. She had a kind smile and smooth brown skin. A name tag was pinned to the open white coat she wore over blue scrubs, but Kae couldn't concentrate long enough to decode the blurry letters.

"Where's my daughter?"

"She's resting—"

"I need to see her."

"You will." The doctor took her hands and her warm, dry skin calmed her. "My name is Dr. Amarita Misra, and I took care of Molly after she was pulled from the wreckage."

Her heart sped up because this statement didn't make any sense. "What wreckage?"

"Sheriff, has no one told her what happened?" the doctor asked Roy.

"She wasn't in the office, so I had to leave a quick message..." He sighed. "I've been dealing with Molly's case since she went missing."

"It doesn't matter." None of this was helping. "I'm here now, can someone tell me what happened?"

"Molly was inside the car that lost control and crashed in front of the hospital," Roy said. "I'm sorry."

"The one that's upside down?" She'd barely spared a glance at the wreckage, or the many people milled around because she only had one thing on her mind. "Molly was in *that* car?" She couldn't grasp what he was saying. "Who was driving?"

"It belonged to... a local woman."

She didn't understand his hesitation. "Why was Molly with her?"

"I don't know."

"Why didn't you ask her? This woman might be the one who abducted her!" The panic was mounting.

"I'm afraid we can't do that," the doctor said.

"Why not?"

"She's in the ICU."

"Who is this woman?"

"Allison Benenati," Roy said.

"What?" Allison lived on her street. She was a mother of three and worked in this hospital's cafeteria. They'd had coffee together many times since Molly's disappearance, and every time Allison offered words of wisdom and prayers that meant nothing to Kae. "That doesn't make any sense."

"Allison's in a coma." Dr. Misra shook her head, sadly. "She's not doing well."

"Is she a suspect?" Her mind was reeling—impossible thoughts whirling too fast to grasp. A shiver raced down her spine, chilling her to the bone.

"Not at the moment," Roy answered.

"Can't you ask Molly what she was doing in Allison's car?" None of this made any damn sense. Her pulse thundered against her temples, threatening to turn into a headache.

"I tried—"

"Molly's not in the ICU as well, is she?" How cruel would the world have to be to steal her daughter away for sixteen months, and then dangle her unconscious in front of her?

"No, she's not." Dr. Misra squeezed her hands. "She was lucky to survive the accident quite unscathed."

"Can I see her?"

"Of course." She raised their joined hands. "But I don't want you to be alarmed when—"

"I thought you said—"

"I know what I said, Mrs.—Kae, but some of her injuries aren't from the accident."

"What do you mean?"

"I think it might be best to show you." The doctor dropped her hands and headed down the white corridor.

Kae snagged Roy's uniform sleeve. "What's happening?" She swallowed the lump wedged in her throat. She wanted answers, not more unanswered questions.

"We don't know yet."

She stared deep into his eyes, to make sure he wasn't lying. It wouldn't be the first time he'd conveniently omitted details to shield her from the awful truth. "You're not keeping anything from me, are you?"

"Of course not." He inched closer, wound an arm around her.

"If you're trying to protect—"

"I wouldn't do that to you, not now. Not with this." He rubbed comforting circles along her spine. A gesture too intimate for this situation.

Usually, his touch helped to keep her centered, would do so much more than that. But while following the doctor down a corridor of uncertainty inside this sterile environment, she wanted to shrug him off. She didn't, because he dropped his arm before she could say anything. Their relationship wasn't a secret, but it wouldn't be right to flaunt their connection during such a dire situation.

Kae was still reeling after finding out her child was in Allison's car. A car that was now lying upside down in the parking lot.

"This is her room." Dr. Misra stopped in front of an open doorway. "As you can see, she's sustained several scratches and required stitches, but she didn't break any bones or suffer a concussion."

Kae wanted to race into the room and scoop Molly up into a motherly embrace, but she stopped in mid motion as soon as she laid eyes on her. She wasn't sure if it was because of her daughter's knotty and singed blonde hair, or the places where the blood hadn't completely been cleaned away from her skin. Maybe it was the horizontal line of stitches across her chest, and down her forearms.

"She looks so fragile." Her sixteen-year-old daughter hadn't appeared this vulnerable since she was a baby. No, she was actually seventeen now because she'd missed her birthday a few months ago.

"She hasn't talked since she got here. Maybe she'll speak to you."

Kae took a step, but hesitated a second time.

"Go on," the doctor said with an encouraging smile. "I imagine you've waited for this moment for a while."

"I have." So, why was she taking her time now?

She took a deep breath and regretted it instantly. The air-conditioned air dried inside her throat. On the exhale, she forced herself to enter the room. "Molly." Her name crackled out of her mouth. The name she'd given her before she was born, now felt foreign.

She didn't respond.

Kae's legs wobbled with every step but she refused to stop now that she'd finally found the courage to move. Not when she was so close to seeing the daughter she'd missed so much. The same one she'd had to accept she might never see again.

But she's alive and she's here.

She stopped beside the bed and stared at her teenage daughter's bruised hands. What had she been through? Where did she go? And how did she end up in a car accident outside their local hospital?

"Molly," she said. "Do you… do you remember me?"

Molly raised her head and slowly turned to face her.

Kae almost recoiled because this girl might look like her daughter, but there was something very different about her. Molly's eyes were blue, but what glared back at her were black pits, hollowed holes full of despair. A cold wind swept up around her, threatening to push her over the edge so these terrible eyes could consume her.

"Kae, are you all right?"

When Roy's hand touched her arm, she jumped. When had he entered the room?

"Is everything okay?"

"Uh…" She blinked, managed a nod. "I'm fine."

He glanced quickly at Molly. "I'm here if you need me."

"Thanks." Kae turned back and found Molly still staring at her, but her eyes were blue. She needed to get more sleep because imagining such creepy things wasn't going to help now that her eldest child was back. "Molly, it's Mom."

"Mom?"

"Yes honey, it's me. I'm so happy you're okay." She hated that her daughter was so confused and physically hurt, but at least she'd come back.

"Mom," she repeated.

"I've missed you so much. We all have." She sat awkwardly on the side of the bed and wrapped her arms around Molly's frail body. "I never stopped looking for you." Molly was nothing more than skin and bones. "I'm so sorry you got lost."

"I wasn't lost," she whispered in her ear.

"Of course, you were. We couldn't find you anywhere." While holding her close, she noticed Molly's hair was brittle and patchy, like wads had been pulled from her scalp. She also smelled strange. An earthy, mossy scent emanated from her and tickled Kae's nose.

She smells like the woods.

Was that where she was all this time? But Roy and his deputies spent months combing the area and didn't find a trace of her.

"I wasn't lost," she repeated. "I went home."

Kae slowly pulled back, but didn't break contact completely. She held on loosely to Molly's sharp elbows, trying not to accidentally touch her injured forearms.

"Honey, someone took you from us."

"That's not true."

"Don't you remember?" Kae couldn't read a single morsel of recognition in her child's eyes. This close, Molly's skin was waxy and too pale. Like someone who'd been kept away from the sun for too long. "You went for a jog early in the morning and didn't..."

She furrowed her brow, and the bruising on her face darkened.

"What did they do to you? Who hurt you?"

"Nobody hurt me."

She wanted to stay strong but couldn't stop the tears any longer. Her daughter was torn and battered, mentally confused. She'd heard about kids who were taken and brainwashed by captors who made them believe impossible things. What did they do to her happy daughter? She couldn't imagine Allison being responsible for any of this. Between her own husband, kids and work, the woman barely had any downtime.

What kind of twisted fuck destroyed Molly's youth and turned her into this... *doll?*

"But, your hair..." She collected her thoughts and feelings long enough to stop the tears. "And your skin... Who cut you up like this?"

"I did," she whispered, pulling out of her grip.

"What?" Molly breaking physical contact made her heart ache, but she needed to stay focused. "What do you mean?"

"I did it." A tiny smile twisted the corners of her dry lips. "To prove myself."

Prove herself to whom? She wanted to confront this head-on but was afraid she might push Molly away. "Whoever did this can't hurt you anymore."

"No... but you can."

"I would never hurt you. I love you."

Molly started trembling, so much the bed vibrated.

"Why were you in the car with Allison?"

She shook her head—left and right, left and right—she didn't stop, didn't answer and the hospital bed wouldn't stop quivering.

"Molly, talk to me." The wheels beneath her screeched. "Tell me what happened."

"No."

"Please."

Molly narrowed her eyes and before Kae could respond, a phantom weight pushed against her chest, shoving her off the bed. She flew across the room until her spine impacted with the opposite wall.

The bed settled back into place.

"Kae!" Roy ran to her side, and the doctor charged into the room.

"Molly..." She couldn't take her eyes off her. Why was she so angry? Did she blame Kae for not finding her sooner? For letting her leave every morning to go jogging in the woods? She'd done the same thing so many times, and came home with her earphones still connected and a sweaty smile on her face. Then one day, she didn't.

Roy helped Kae get to her feet.

"What happened?"

"I don't know." She watched her daughter's eyes blink from blue to black, and that sly smile was back on her face.

"Let's get you out of here."

"No, Roy. I don't want to leave her."

He tightened his grip on her arms. "We have to let the doctor and nurses do their job—"

"But I just got her back."

"I know, and she's not going anywhere. I'm putting a deputy outside this room to keep watch over her."

She dared to look away. "You promise?"

"Of course." He pulled her close.

The doctor was leaning over Molly as Roy led Kae out of the room. She wasn't sure what was happening but Molly's eyes were closed and she was slumped against the pillow.

Molly reminded her of a discarded rag doll.

DAY TWO

Wednesday
November 11, 2015

3:00am

"Hey, Kae." Roy called from the bed. "What're you doing?"

"The rain woke me." The rain striking the window across the room did wake her, but she wasn't exactly sleeping soundly at the time. Too many uncomfortable thoughts were tumbling inside her brain and chased her into a series of heavy nightmares.

He patted the mattress. "Come back to bed."

"I can't." She couldn't stop thinking about what happened at the hospital. The condition her daughter was in, the weird things she'd seen—black eyes, shaky bed, a phantom weight—and Molly's anger.

"Come here and I'll—"

"I can't deal with losing her all over again."

The sheets rustled, filling the silence while complementing the constant rain. She felt his approach and when he wrapped his arms around her, she leaned into his warm chest. The contact with his bare skin soothed her nerves. If not for this man, she would have surrendered into the abyss of grief a long time ago.

"You're not going to lose her," he whispered into her hair.

"She doesn't remember me." Kae looked out the window to focus on the swelling puddles outside rather than the fact she hadn't detected an ounce of recognition in her daughter's vacant eyes. The way Molly told her *she* was the one who could hurt her, not whoever had taken her away from her life, still burned inside. Hurt soul-deep.

"She's obviously been through a lot." He tightened his arms around her. "Victims of abductions suffer a great deal of trauma from their experience. She could have amnesia, or PTSD—probably both."

"I understand all that, but there was something different about her."

"Kae, I know this is going to be hard to accept, but Molly will probably never be the same girl she was before all of this." His tone was soft and caring, but the words still stabbed like daggers inside her already wounded heart.

"I just…" She sighed. "I want to help her."

"And you will."

"I'm her mother for fuck's sake, and she told me *I'm* the one who can hurt her. That she went home, instead of vanishing into thin air for sixteen fucking months."

He kissed the top of her head. "Don't let what she said get to you. She's confused, and the accident probably added to her disorientation."

"What do you think happened?" She desperately wanted to understand the disconnected pieces of her daughter's disappearance and return.

"I don't know." Roy's breath stirred her messy hair. "I spoke to Anthony earlier, and he confirmed Allison headed out to work at the same time she always did."

"How's he holding up?"

"He's concerned and confused, doesn't know what to tell the kids."

She hated that someone else had gotten hurt because of all this.

While deep in thought, Ray loosened his grip and Kae turned in his embrace until they were facing each other.

"Do you think she'll ever remember me?" She'd lost her daughter on a summer morning, and a stranger had returned this winter.

"I think she will." He wrapped his arms around her waist. "But there's nothing we can do to make her. She needs time to find herself again."

"I know, but…"

"Kae, I need you to do something for me."

"What?"

"I need you to promise that you won't let her words hurt you. Right now, she's confused, disoriented—she was involved in a car accident. We don't know what she went through before that, or how she got away. Our questions are only going to rattle her, maybe push her toward her kidnapper if she developed any sort of attachment."

His eyes were shiny and full of concern. Sometimes she didn't think she deserved this good and kind man, and hated that they'd reconnected during one of the hardest times in her life. He was too good for all of this uncertainty, but she couldn't bring herself to push him away. She loved him too much. Always had.

"I'll try."

"I'm sure she'll remember you because you're very hard to forget," he said. "Trust me, I know."

"You're too sweet for all of this crap. I'm sorry—"

"Hey, don't ever say or think that." He cupped her face in his hands and leaned closer to meet her gaze. "I didn't stick by you so you'd feel bad. I'm with you because I want to be here, because the only person who could make me leave is you."

"I'm not letting you go." His face blurred because she couldn't stop the overwhelming emotions he stirred inside her. "I'm sorry if going through this is dredging up bad memories for you. You're the only person who truly understands what I'm going through."

Unlike Molly, his son Billy was found a week after he vanished.

"Don't be. I've made my peace with what happened to Billy."

As brave as she knew he was, Sheriff Roy Everly lost his twelve-year-old son six years before, when the boy went into the woods and never came home. Kae knew this must be hard to deal with, and probably unearthed too many painful memories. Not only about Billy, but his partner leaving Thicket because she couldn't deal with all the reminders. He'd stayed, and fate had reconnected him with Kae when she'd suffered her own version of a similar tragedy.

That they'd fallen in love all over again during all the sadness and turmoil was the only light in her life during the past year.

"I owe you a debt I'll never be able to repay."

"You don't owe me anything." He leaned even closer, until their lips were a mere inch away. "You never did, and never will. I love you."

"I love you so much." She smiled at him, but the tears blurred his handsome face. The same face she'd loved when they were the inseparable teenage couple who'd spent the last two years of high school together. Until they decided to go their separate ways. Kae went off to college and when she came back, found he was a deputy and was living with someone else.

"Don't cry, we'll make it through together. I promise."

She exhaled, trying to push the tears away while managing a quick nod.

One by one, he kissed her tears away. Until his mouth suddenly covered hers and she found herself melting into his kiss. Their mouths stayed together even when he scooped her up into his arms and laid her down on the bed. It wasn't until there was a beep on his phone that he reluctantly stopped.

Roy sighed. "I better check that."

"Yeah," she said, breathless.

He leaned over her and she caressed his tight abdomen as he recovered his cell phone, but she stopped when he frowned.

"What's going on?"

Roy stared at the screen for another second before he said, "There's a strange text here from the deputy I left outside Molly's room."

Her heart skipped a beat. "Strange, how?"

"Well, for starters, it just came through but it's dated over an hour ago."

"The reception around here can be spotty sometimes…"

"He also said he was going to check on something and get back to me right away, but he didn't."

"What did he have to check?"

"I don't know." He dialed and the ringtone echoed in the silence once, twice, three times—all the way to ten. "He's not answering."

"Maybe he fell asleep."

He hung up and dialed again, but got the same response. He dialed another number. "Yes, hello, this is Sheriff Everly. I'm trying to get in touch with the deputy outside Molly Roscoe's room and he's not answering. Yes, I'll hold."

Time stretched and weighed more than it should, and she couldn't stop her nerves from cramping up.

"Yes, I'm here. Okay. Are you sure he's not in the room?" Roy was quiet for a moment before he nodded, thanked the nurse and said he'd be right over.

"What's wrong?"

"The nurse can't find him. The chair's still there, but he's not in the room."

"And Molly?"

"She's asleep."

"What do you think happened?"

"Maybe he's taking a toilet break. We'll wait a few minutes and I'll try again." But after five, the officer still didn't answer. Roy sighed as he rolled out of bed. "I'm going to check on him, to make sure he's all right."

She didn't like him leaving in the middle of the night, but what choice did she have?

As Roy got dressed into his uniform, she wondered why life had to get in the way of all the good bits.

"Are you going to be all right on your own?"

"I'm not alone, the twins are here."

He nodded before leaning over for another deep and meaningful kiss. "Come and lock up, then please try to get some rest."

"I can't rest until I hear from you."

"This isn't another burden for you to—"

"The guy was watching over my daughter, so I think it is."

"I won't even try to change your mind. At least try to relax."

Kae followed him into the darkened hallway, down the stairs and stopped at the front door. She stood on her tiptoes and kissed him again and told him to be careful before she locked the door. Kae watched out the side window until his car left the wet driveway, and when she turned around to head back to bed, her heart leaped into her throat.

Molly was standing in the corridor, staring at her. What was she doing here? And why was she bleeding droplets onto the floor?

"Molly?" Her voice quivered.

"Mama."

Molly always calls me Mom. Or at least, she used to before she'd switched to Mother.

She flicked the overhead light. "What's wrong, honey?"

When Molly stepped out of the shadows, she morphed into her younger sister.

"Tessa… what are you doing up?" How could she have mistaken her youngest for her oldest?

"I had a bad dream and needed a drink of water."

"Why are you wet?" The droplets she'd spotted weren't blood, they were raindrops.

"Thought I heard something outside—"

"Please, don't ever go outside in the middle of the night. Ever." She couldn't stand the thought of another one of her children vanishing into thin air.

"I know, but the dream confused me…"

"What was your dream about?" She'd always tried to make the kids recall their nightmares so they could overcome their fear.

"The creepy tree man was calling me again."

"What creepy tree man?" Her blood chilled and gooseflesh spread over her skin. "And what do you mean by again?"

"I didn't tell you because I didn't want you to freak out." Tessa sighed. "And Other Mother said it was probably best not to scare you."

Other Mother, aka Sofia, her ex-husband's young wife. The name the twins started calling her because they both loved the book *Coraline* and pretended they were going to an alternate world every time they stayed with their father.

The thought of another woman telling one of her kids to keep secrets from her made Kae's blood boil.

"You should tell me anything you want to tell me, especially if it scares you and you're having dreams about it. We've always faced our nightmares together."

Tessa didn't meet her eyes.

"Who is this tree *monster?*"

"The horned man made out of bark and leaves," Tessa whispered, glancing at the window beside the front door. "His fiery eyes are shiny and he promises to take me home."

"*This* is your home." Her skin crawled because—minus the tree man—this sounded like a similar version of what Molly said to her in the hospital. "You don't have to worry about some creepy nightmare man, you're safe here."

"I know, Mama. It was just a bad dream."

"You better try and get some sleep."

"I will. Good night."

Kae's nerves were still on edge. There was definitely something in the air, and it was more than winter reaching its frosty fingers into what was left of fall.

Maybe she should stop concentrating on negative things and focus on the good stuff. Molly was absent last November, but she would be here for Thanksgiving this year. That was something worth getting excited about. She might even consider inviting Devin and Sofia so they could all celebrate together, instead of in shifts. Of course, Roy would come too.

The thought of him being in every celebration from now on made up for all the other terrible feelings quivering inside.

She stayed where she was for a while, trying to focus on positive thoughts. But she couldn't stop thinking about Tessa, because she knew that bad dreams sometimes came true.

3:33am

Roy Everly parked his cruiser and fast-walked across the parking lot. The rain was heavier now and the crisp air almost cut off his breath. Winter wouldn't officially arrive until next month, but the chill was already creeping into his bones.

The last thing he'd wanted to do in the early hours of the morning was to leave Kae's warm bed when she'd finally allowed herself to relax a little, but he couldn't ignore the tingling on the back of his neck. The sixth sense that told him something was very wrong.

As he closed the distance, unable to keep the rain from drenching his shirt, his heart ached for Kae.

Even after Molly's unexpected return, she was still caught in a tangled web of emotional turmoil. He knew how hard it was to get off that damned roller-coaster of emotions, so Roy would do whatever he could to help ease her pain and uncertainty.

He craned his neck to glance at the white building and spotted a shadow standing in front of one of the dimly-lit rooms. He could've sworn someone was staring at him from the other side. A shiver ran down the length of his spine. Why would anyone be watching the parking lot in front of the hospital in the wee hours of the morning?

I desperately need some real sleep.

The appeal of Kae's warm and comfortable bed never sounded more ideal. Even if he found his deputy quickly, he couldn't go back. Refused to disrupt her and possibly interrupt the kids.

As much as he'd tried to ease Kae's mind, he couldn't deny that this situation was affecting him too, playing havoc with his head. There was something off about Molly but he couldn't pinpoint what. He'd noticed the dirt on the girl's body, the blood pouring from multiple wounds. The smeared rusty stains and the awful stitching across her chest and down her arms. He'd noticed the cuts on her lips and brow, how pale she was.

He'd questioned Molly as soon as the doctor and nurses cleaned her up, redid the stitches and tucked her away in the safety of her own room. Dr. Misra insisted it was best to keep her isolated, to fight off confusion or hostility. Not that it ended up helping with either.

The teenager hadn't answered any of his questions and refused to look at him. He couldn't erase the image of Kae being propelled across the room when she'd tried to comfort her. He'd never seen anything like it. One second, she was sitting on the edge of the bed, the next she was in the air.

There's something really strange going on around here.

And he needed to get to the bottom of it.

The fact his team had spent months searching the woods for clues and failed to find anything but earphones and a hoodie, troubled him immensely. At least his son was found a week later, discarded like a piece of meat.

No, don't go there. This path leads to pain.

Roy pushed the haunting thoughts away and was about to reach the automatic doors when a lump fell from the sky. He stopped in time to watch the mass land with a squelching thump, spewing a combination of blood and rain onto his pants.

"What the hell?"

The deputy he'd come to track down was now a lump of bloody meat on the pavement. He was still wearing his uniform, with name-tag and gun belt attached, but his face was an unrecognizable mess.

Someone screamed and the automatic doors opened to reveal two paramedics heading out for the night. The pair paused when they spotted the fleshy heap and rushed to the fallen officer seconds after they registered what lay on the concrete.

Roy managed to push away the shock and called the incident in. He needed backup, not only to clean this up and patrol the area, but to help search the clinic. It might be three in the morning and raining, but a hospital was always busy.

"What happened?" the shorter paramedic asked.

"I don't know, he—"

"I saw him jump!" whoever stood close behind him said.

Roy turned and found a distraught balding man with a makeshift bandage wrapped around his hand.

"You actually saw him jump?" He'd been too busy wondering why anyone would be at the window at this hour. While trying to avoid painful memories from resurfacing.

"He was on the roof, waving at someone," he said. "And then he jumped."

Had Blackwell tried to get his attention? The thought made him uneasy. Why hadn't he noticed him? Had he been so lost in restless thoughts his instincts failed him?

"Is he alive?" He doubted anyone could survive such a fall, but wanted to hear it from the professionals.

The paramedic shook her head.

"I've got backup coming." The world was slipping away from him but it was essential to hold on. He was the Sheriff and had to clean this up. He couldn't bring himself to look at Deputy Steven Blackwell.

"We won't touch anything until the scene has been cleared." The male paramedic stood near his partner.

The bleating of sirens was shortly followed by two police cars screeching to a halt near the entrance. Roy rushed to meet them.

Deputy Betty Tran climbed out of the closest vehicle. "What happened?"

"Looks like a suicide, but we can't be sure." He stepped in front of her before she could get any closer. "He's one of ours."

Her eyes widened, but she nodded as her lips thinned.

"I need you to take a statement from that guy. He witnessed the jump." He glanced at the guy's bandage. The man was clearly hurt and shaken. "Actually,. make sure he gets to the ER first, and *then* take his statement."

She glanced at his pants.

"You can get my statement later. I need to get inside to make sure the person Blackwell was guarding is okay."

"The Roscoe girl?" The shine of suspicion flashed in her eyes. "I'll go and take care of the statement."

"Soule, I need you to check the area," he instructed his other deputy, Mike Soule.

"Yes, sir."

Roy backtracked enough to leave the commotion of the entrance so he could check out the roof. Standing near the edge was a girl. *Molly.* Her hospital gown danced in the wind but her hair hung limp like a curtain shielding her features.

He was about to call out for her to step away from the edge, but she was already gone. Was he seeing things tonight? Maybe he should take his own advice and get some rest. But not yet, he had something to do first.

Roy charged into the hospital. He bypassed the elevators and took the stairs two at a time while pulling out his Smith & Wesson M&P. He was fit and reached the fourth floor without being winded by the time he pushed open the door.

The fluorescent lights dimmed over his head. The one outside Molly's room was completely dark. The vacant chair sat beside the open door, with a thin book lying open on the seat. He recalled the last time he'd teased Blackwell about his addiction to the dusty and damaged pulp science fiction paperbacks he found in garage sales and charity stores.

He'll never read another one, and didn't get the chance to finish this one.

His chest constricted. Losing a fellow officer didn't get easier with experience.

Roy strode gun-first into the room and was hit by a wall of ice. The frosty air washed over him, so fast his skin goose-pimpled.

"Molly." His own voice sounded far away. As if he was outside himself and not quite connected to his surroundings. With every new step, the temperature dropped until the room was colder than the night outside.

Curling swirls of smoke filled the dark corners and skittering filled his ears.

He tilted his head toward the ceiling and pointed the gun at... nothing. He could've sworn he'd spotted several humanoid shadows—because he couldn't think of a better way to describe what his mind was trying to convey—crawling upside down like spiders. Cold sweat dripped into his eyes and after rubbing the liquid away with his free hand, the room shifted back to normal.

Everything was in its place, and the temperature leveled out.

It took several seconds to settle his nerves and realize he'd reached Molly's bedside. He lowered the S&W.

She was asleep, her eyelids quivered and both of her arms lay at her sides, in restraints. The straps couldn't hide the vertical lines of stitching on both forearms, or the droplets of blood staining her hospital gown.

How had she gotten blood on her? And if she was still strapped to the bed, how could he have seen her on the roof?

Molly's head swiveled around like a marionette being manipulated by an invisible puppet master, and her eyes were identical hollows of darkness. He was caught in her glare, and the compulsion to slip into the abyss made him step closer.

The longer he stared, the more he could see inside these black pits. Skittering dusky shadows with long limbs slithering inside her, thin fingers reaching from the inside of her eye sockets ready to claim him if he let them.

"Is everything okay?"

Roy turned and found a nurse in the illuminated doorway. It took him a minute to compose himself, but he managed to clear his throat and said, "I'm checking to make sure she's all right."

"I was about to do the same." She strolled into the room. "Just heard about what happened."

"Are you the nurse I spoke to on the phone?"

"Yes." She grabbed the chart from the end of the bed and rifled through the pages. "After speaking to you I checked the rest of the ward, but I couldn't find the young man anywhere."

"Did you notice him slipping away?"

"To be honest, no. He was busy reading and I was working on paperwork." She made her way to the other side of the bed to check Molly's pulse. "Whoa, you might want to lower that, Sheriff."

"What?"

"Your gun."

Roy blinked several times when he found the butt of his weapon was dangerously close to his temple. When had he done that? He dropped his arm and secured his sidearm back into the holster.

"How's she doing?"

"She's doing very well, considering. All her vitals are good. The abrasions and bruises seem to be healing without infection. We're waiting for the bloodwork to come back, to make sure everything checks out." She scribbled on the chart. "Her only problem is her refusal to eat or speak. And what she did to her mother, of course."

He nodded, not eager to get into that uncomfortable conversation. "Do you think she'll be released soon?"

"That depends on Dr. Misra." The nurse shrugged. "Can I help you with anything else?"

"No. At least, for now," he said. "I'll get out of the way."

"I'm sorry about the deputy."

"I appreciate that."

Roy paused when he reached the doorway and surveyed the room one last time, but he couldn't find a single shifting shadow or the menace he'd felt only minutes ago.

9:00am

"Hey, I've been trying to call you for hours." Kae sat in her idling car outside the local middle school after morning drop off. She was relieved one of her calls had finally connected.

"Sorry I couldn't call," Roy said. "It's been crazy around here—"

"Did something happen to Molly?"

"No, she's fine."

"I've been going out of my mind with worry." Roy had left the house hours ago and didn't call, so she'd kept busy getting the twins ready for school.

"Deputy Blackwell died."

Her pulse sped up. "The officer you put outside Molly's room?"

"Yes."

"Was someone trying to get to—"

"No, nothing like that." He sighed and it echoed down the line. "Hold on a sec." The sound of muffled background activity was replaced by silence. "Sorry about that, I can't talk for long."

"What happened to him?"

"It's all speculation, but he either fell or jumped off the roof of the hospital," he said. "Right in front of me."

"Oh my God." She didn't know what else to say. "I'm so sorry."

"It's been a shit morning full of statements, reports and talking to the ME."

"Does anyone know why he would jump?"

"Not yet. His parents are devastated and so far, I don't see the picture of a suicidal police officer fitting this scenario."

"What do you think happened?"

"I have no idea, but there's some strange shit going on around here and I intend to get to the bottom of it."

"Is there anything I can do to help?"

"No, you have enough to worry about and need to concentrate on your daughter." There was something in his voice. "You have the rest of the week off, right?"

"Yeah." As soon as she'd heard about Molly, she'd begged her boss to give her the week off. "When can I see you?"

"I'll be busy most of the day, but I'll call or text you as soon as I can."

"Maybe you can actually stay the whole night this time," she said, hoping to inject a tiny bit of positivity into such a bleak situation. At least the rain was light and spotty now, had poured most if its rage in the early hours of the morning.

"I hope so."

"And Roy."

"Yeah?"

"I'm really sorry."

"Thanks," he said. "I have to go."

"Okay." She didn't want to hang up, had a bad feeling about disconnecting the call and couldn't explain why.

"Kae!"

"Yeah?"

"I love you."

"Love you too."

She lowered the cellphone away from her ear when Roy disconnected the call, and stared at the wallpaper of her three kids during the last Christmas they'd spent together. Molly appeared so much younger and so did the twins. They'd enjoyed a lovely morning together, opening presents and listening to Christmas carols as the snow thickened outside. Molly had been looking forward to lunchtime, when their father would pick them up and take the kids to his place so they could do the present-opening all over again.

Molly never got over the divorce, and had resented Kae because she blamed her for Devin leaving them. But she was a kid and didn't understand adult relationships, or that her father's wandering eye was the reason why their marriage fell apart.

She dumped the phone on the passenger seat and sighed. She tried to calm her nerves and started the engine, ready to head for the hospital.

Kae couldn't believe a young deputy had died where Molly was currently staying. Not just that, but he was the one who was supposed to be watching her room. Now, Roy had his hands full, and was probably suffering alone. His fellow officers were like family to him, and he'd often spoken about Steven in a very fond way.

She tried to concentrate on the slick road and not on all this sadness. Life was already dangerous, without adding terrible weather conditions to the mix.

After only a few street turns, she couldn't stop herself from thinking about what happened in the hospital room yesterday. But she had to stay strong. Needed to support Molly, as well as maintain an air of normalcy for the twins.

Kae took a left into St. Jude's parking lot and maneuvered her car into the first available spot. She switched off the ignition and pocketed the key. She gasped when she glanced in the rearview mirror.

"Don't be alarmed," the guy sitting in the backseat said.

"Steven?" Her breath misted in front of her. She'd met the deputy several times, and knew this was him.

"Yeah."

"But how? I thought…"

"I don't understand this either," he said. "Don't much understand anything that's been going on lately, to be honest."

"What are you doing in my car?"

"I don't think I'm really here."

The interior was freezing and her lips were going numb. "Then why can I see you?"

He shrugged.

She kept her eyes glued to the rearview mirror. "If you're… gone, that makes you a ghost. Have you come to tell me something?" She'd watched enough movies to know this had to be the case, but never expected to experience this herself.

"Tell Sheriff Everly that I was pushed."

"Who pushed you?"

Steven didn't answer, but his dark reflected eyes were stuck on hers.

Between blinks, he was gone.

She swiveled around but he wasn't in the backseat and had disappeared from the mirror.

Kae grabbed her cell, bag and left the car. It wasn't until she was halfway across the parking lot that she wondered if she'd even locked the door.

The rain drizzled on her hair and face but she didn't feel anything. She was numb and wanted space from what she'd witnessed. How could she tell Roy she'd received a visit from the ghost of his deputy without sounding like someone suffering from obvious trauma?

The thought made her pause. For all she knew, she might have imagined the young man. She shuddered at the thought but quickened her step when she spotted her ex-husband waiting near the automated doors. He was busy sucking on the end of a cigarette.

"Those things are going to kill you," she said.

"You gotta die of something."

"That wasn't funny when we were married, and it still isn't."

Devin narrowed his eyes as he sucked the cancer stick dry. "That's probably why our marriage didn't work, because you never found me funny."

"No," she said, storming past him. "It didn't work because you decided to get involved with someone else."

"You're never going to get over that, are you?"

"I'm glad you at least had the decency to come to the hospital alone." She couldn't see Sofia anywhere, and she was glad. After what Tessa told her, she didn't trust herself around the woman.

"Sofia's waiting in the car."

"How nice," she said. "Like a loyal puppy."

"You're in a nasty mood today."

Kae turned to face him and because they were about the same height, she pointed a finger at his face. "You think I'm nasty today, huh? Our daughter has been missing for over a year and although she's returned, we still don't know where she's been or what happened to her. And during all that time you barely spoke to me. Most of the time, you couldn't even bring yourself to knock on the door when you picked the kids up."

The betrayal of him waiting in the driveway or sending his wife to the door to pick up the twins still stung. For all of Kae's suspicions about Sofia, at least she'd taken the time to ask how she was doing.

"Hey, that's not fair. I took the kids whenever you—"

"You took the kids because they're *your* children too, and the courts ordered you to."

"Damn it, Kae, you know that's not true." His eyes were full of anger or hurt, she couldn't tell the difference anymore.

Several people skirted past, and the anger drained out of her. This wasn't the time or place to have this ancient fight. Between Molly's return, Tessa's strange behavior, and seeing the man Roy told her was dead, she'd been shaken to the core.

"I'm sorry, okay?" Devin ran a hand through his thinning hair. "I can't believe they finally found her. I'm so glad, but amazed. You know?"

Kae sighed. "Come on, let's go and see how she's doing."

He nodded and followed her to the elevators.

Sometimes, Kae found it was hard to believe she'd actually married this vain and emotionally-vacant man, to remember they'd met in a bar and had fallen in love. Truth was, she'd often questioned if she'd ever truly loved Devin the way she'd convinced herself she had. At the time, fresh out of college and back in Thicket, she'd filled herself with delusions of rekindling her relationship with Roy, but he'd moved on and was already living with someone. Meeting Devin in that smoky bar was convenient, and although love might have taken some self-convincing, she'd certainly fallen in lust with Devin. The older man who rode around on a motorcycle and actually noticed her. But it hadn't taken long for them to start drifting apart, for her to believe that when she fell pregnant with the twins, the babies might be the salvation their relationship desperately needed.

Tessa and Tommy were a miracle, but they couldn't salvage a doomed marriage. Not long after their births, Devin started an affair with one of his students. The man was a cliché through and through. The worst thing was, Kae hadn't much cared about his betrayal and was glad to see him leave.

At least he'd never turned his back on the kids. It was why they all loved him so much and enjoyed spending time at his house. Why Molly idolized her father. At least, she had before.

They took the elevator up to the fourth floor in silence, and she wondered what he was thinking about. When the doors opened, she led the way down the white corridor. She stopped in the doorway and ushered him in.

"Dad!"

"Hey baby, it's so good to see you." He covered the length of the room in three strides and was hugging his teenage daughter in seconds.

Kae followed, cautious about Molly's reaction. As she surveyed the room, she spotted Sienna and Mew sitting on the other side of the bed. Who told them where to find her? She suddenly felt like the worst kind of person because it hadn't occurred to her to call either one of these kids. Even though they periodically turned up at the house to check on her, and asked if there was any news about Molly. These two kids were her daughter's friends and Kae had forgotten all about them.

"Hi, Mrs. Roscoe."

"Ms.—"

"You still haven't changed your name, huh?" Devin teased. "I don't mind."

"It's only a matter of time," she said. "Hello, Sienna, Mew. What're you kids doing here? Shouldn't you be at school?"

"We have a free period," Sienna said, although she was obviously lying.

Kae nodded, didn't want to interrogate them. "How are you feeling today, Molly?"

"Good." She avoided her eyes, while clutching her father's hand.

She took a deep breath and reached out to pat Molly's other arm but she stiffened at the contact and shrugged her off. Kae attempted to hide the hurt, but her ex was watching.

"I've missed you so much," Devin said, sitting on the side of the bed.

Kae noticed the temporary restraints the doctor told her were necessary had been removed.

"I missed you too."

"Where were you?" he asked.

Silence filled the room. No matter how many times someone asked this question, Molly didn't answer.

"I'm not sure." Molly shook her head. "It's all a bit foggy."

"But it's been so long since you disappeared."

Kae wanted to cut in, to warn him about pushing her.

"Were you taken by someone?"

"I don't know," she whispered.

"How did you get away?"

"I didn't."

Kae stepped closer. "Devin—"

"Molly, that doesn't make any sense." He leaned closer, trying to catch her eye. "I want to know what happened to my daughter."

She yanked her hand from his. "I just told you. *I don't know.*"

"Devin—"

"You have to try to remember, so we can help—"

"No!" The bed rattled and the wheels screeched.

"Jesus." Devin slipped off the bed and bumped into Kae.

"I'm sorry, I…"

"It's okay." She grabbed a hold of his arm and led him away from the rattling bed. "Trust me, it's not a good idea to push her. I found out the hard way."

"That's not good enough." His eyes flashed and he returned to the bed. "Molly, we're worried about you. We want to help."

The bed stopped suddenly. "Oh, Daddy, you don't need to worry."

"But—"

"Everything's going to be okay now that I'm back." Her smile was too wide and didn't meet her eyes, made her look like a leering marionette.

Devin considered her for several quiet moments before nodding. "Okay, fine. But if you need to talk, you know you can call me any time."

"I know."

Dr. Misra entered the room with a smile on her face. "Looks like we have a full house today."

"Good morning, Doctor."

"Good morning to you, Kae." Her smile was positively beaming. "Has my favorite patient told you she started eating again?"

"No." Kae glanced at her daughter, but her eyes were focused on her friends. The two youngsters sat still in their chairs, with eyes glued to Molly's in what appeared to be a hypnotic trance.

"Well, she's eating and her vitals are excellent." The doctor smiled at Devin. "Hello, and who might you be?"

"I'm Molly's father."

"This is my ex-husband, Devin."

"It's nice to meet you." They shook hands. "Your daughter is in good hands and if she gets some proper rest, she can go home later on."

"Really?" The thought made Kae happy, yet uneasy.

"That's great news!" Devin said with a huge grin.

"Am I going home with you, Dad?"

Devin opened his mouth to respond, but Kae cut in. "Molly, you live with me and your brother and sister."

"But I want to go and live with Daddy."

Devin went to her side, placed a hand on her shoulder. "Just because you'll be going home with your mother doesn't mean you won't come and stay with me, too."

"With you and Sofia?"

Kae's heart sank into her stomach. How did she remember Devin's wife by name but had trouble recalling her own mother? She lowered her head and swallowed back the tears because she refused to let anyone see her pain.

"Of course! Sofia can't wait to see you."

Molly beamed at the news. "Promise?"

He kissed the top of her head. "I promise."

"Aren't you looking forward to seeing your brother and sister?" Kae threw out her last ray of hope. Maybe her siblings might mean more to her than her own mother.

She shrugged.

Kae folded her arms over her stomach to keep the impulse to slap some sense into Molly from manifesting. She despised the compulsion as soon as it struck and hoped no one noticed.

"Okay, that's enough excitement for today," Dr. Misra called with a clap of her hands. "Molly needs to get some rest."

Kae kissed her cold cheek. "I'll come back later."

"Don't bother," she whispered.

Kae's vision blurred with unshed tears, but she blinked them away as she left the room with the others in tow. This time she didn't bother to look back, but watched Sienna and Mew take the stairs without so much as a wave.

"Will she ever remember what happened to her?" Devin asked as the trio headed towards the nurse's station.

"It's hard to say," the doctor said.

"I hope she does because whoever did this to my daughter needs to pay." Devin's tone was menacing. "She has clumps of hair missing, a jagged cut across her chest and down her arms. I—we—need to find out what happened to her."

"I know the injuries look bad, but it's mostly cosmetic. We cleaned all of her wounds and re-stitched—"

Kae stopped to face them. "Re-stitched?" In her haste to see Molly the day before and being sidelined, she now realized she hadn't asked any real questions.

Dr. Misra nodded. "When we found her in the car, the stitches across her chest and arms were done with what appeared to be… vines, or grass."

"Vines?" Devin echoed. "What the hell does that mean?"

"I'm not sure yet, but we've sent them to the lab for analysis."

"This is so fucked up."

"Yes, Mr. Roscoe, it is." Dr. Misra nodded sympathetically. "But you can't push her, because if you do, she might close off completely. Or, could fabricate stories about her experience. It's best to concentrate on her health and well-being, to show her as much love as you can."

"That's a little hard when she flinches at my touch." Kae didn't feel proud of her outburst, but it was now in the open for a health professional to sift through.

"I noticed her aggression toward you, but I wouldn't take it personally."

"Why does she shun away from me, but welcomed her father?"

"Probably because of my charm," he said.

"More than likely it's because the primary caregiver is usually the target for anger and resentment." Dr. Misra's eyes softened. "She was gone a long time, and you couldn't find her. Now that she's back, her anger could be manifesting in acts of cruelty because she feels like her mother abandoned her."

"What? I never gave up hope!"

The doctor raised a hand between them. "I realize that, Kae, but Molly's still recovering from an ordeal none of us know anything about."

"Will she overcome this... resentment?" Kae wasn't sure she could deal with her daughter's unrelenting cruelty. They'd had disagreements in the past but this was new, callous territory. She'd almost broken down inside the room, and hadn't been able to stop her outburst.

"She needs time. We can't rush her, and everyone's different so we can't guess at her reaction time." The doctor placed a hand on her arm. "But please, don't take it to heart. Your daughter's lost and confused right now. She might not act like it, but she needs you."

"I don't know what to do."

"All you can do is be there for her, listen and pay attention."

She wanted to ask what would happen if Molly never remembered their time together, but bit her tongue.

"I better get back to my rounds. But if you have any questions—either of you—feel free to contact me." Dr. Misra smiled, waved and headed down the opposite direction.

"She's a ball of sunshine that one," Devin said. "I don't know how she does it, working in such a miserable place."

"Yeah."

"Hey, don't worry about Molly, okay?" He draped an arm around her shoulder as they headed for the elevator. "You know how she is. Remember when she didn't speak to you for two weeks because you didn't let her go on an amusement park tour with me?"

"It was during the school year."

He rolled his eyes as they walked into the elevator and she ducked out of his grasp.

She smacked the button to the lobby too hard and hurt her finger, but she didn't care.

"Why did you roll your eyes?" she snapped.

"I don't want to get into another argument with you, okay?"

The doors opened and she stormed out.

"Kae, wait!"

She ignored him and crossed the hospital foyer as fast as she could manage without slipping on the random puddles. She raced out and breathed in the frigid air, happy for the cold and the drizzly rain. She didn't stop when he followed her outside calling after her, didn't bother to look back and picked up her pace.

She'd put up with Molly's behavior because their daughter was ripped away from her life for sixteen months, but she refused to put up with Devin's bullshit.

Kae was grateful to find the car door was locked as she climbed inside and got the engine running. She peeked into the rearview mirror to reverse out of the spot, and gasped.

"You can't leave yet," Steven said.

"What?"

"He's on the roof."

"Who's on the roof?"

"Sheriff Everly."

She was still trying to catch her breath and was having trouble deciphering what he was trying to tell her.

"He's in danger."

Her heart skipped a beat. "Are you telling me that Roy's on the roof right now?"

Steven nodded.

Before her mind caught up with her heart, Kae was already back out in the rain. She pulled her phone out of her pocket and dialed his number, but it rang out. Damn the shitty connection in this town. She kept trying as she jogged through the parking lot. If Roy was at the hospital, surely there were other cops around too. Hadn't she noticed one or two in the foyer earlier, maybe on Molly's floor? She couldn't remember.

As Kae approached the entrance, she stopped when she saw Roy exactly where Steven told her he would be. He was standing on the roof, but shadows appeared out of nowhere and wrapped themselves around his body, raising him.

She watched in horror as he fell over the side and was left dangling from the building.

"Roy!" she yelled, but the wind carried her voice away. "Shit."

She ran into the hospital, determined to find someone who could help.

10:33am

The wind and rain whipped Roy's shaggy hair into his eyes but he didn't bother to wipe it away. He took his time across the hospital's roof, his shoes splashing into puddles, while he inspected his surroundings.

He was hoping to find some sort of clue about what happened to Deputy Blackwell in the early hours of this morning. If the young deputy was supposed to be watching Molly, how did he end up here?

An image wound its way into his mind—Molly standing on the edge of this very roof when Roy was headed for the entrance. She'd vanished, but what if *she* was the reason the deputy was on the roof? What if he'd chased her to this very spot?

Roy spotted a few droplets of black goo in the puddles, but didn't know what it could be. Not with this weather destroying any evidence.

He reached the edge and leaned forward to inspect the ground below. Even though his eyesight wasn't perfect and the rain had thankfully helped wash away most of the carnage, he knew where the officer's battered body had landed.

Who pushed him, and why?

He'd gone through the kid's apartment and hadn't found any clear indication that he was suffering from mental illness serious enough to take his own life. Actually, he'd found out Steven was seeing a girl he'd met online a few months ago, and planned to meet up with her again this weekend.

No, he wasn't buying the suicide angle.

As convenient as it would be to pin this investigation on the most obvious answer, he refused to do so until he found a real motive. He didn't believe Blackwell jumped, especially after reading the bald man's statement. Like Roy, the witness thought he'd spotted someone standing behind the deputy. Then again, the man did admit to taking medication before leaving his house.

"What happened?" The wind coiled around his body like an invisible force tightening its grip.

His foot slid on the slippery concrete, propelling him headfirst toward the edge. His heart pounded hard and fast as he tried to right himself, but he couldn't stop his feet from being raised off the ground. No matter how hard he tried to fight, he was heading in one direction—over.

No!

His life couldn't end like this. He had so much living left to do, and there was Kae to consider. He'd wanted her for so long and now that they were finally together, he didn't want to leave her. To devastate her even more than she already was.

The force thrust him with so much vigor, he tipped over the side.

He raised his right arm in time to catch the concrete lip before falling to his untimely death. Gripping the slick surface hurt like a son of a bitch and his fingers were already slipping. Rain was dripping into his eyes and his shoulder was probably separating, but he held on tight. He lifted his other arm and swung forward, slamming his chest hard against the stucco wall so he was left dangling from the side of the building.

The impact winded him but he didn't let go.

A scream from below made him quake and he almost lost his grip. Someone had seen him, but he hoped no one chased him up here because he didn't want to put anyone else in danger.

Roy took a deep breath and regretted it. The wind flew up his nose too fast, overfilling his lungs. If he didn't calm the fuck down, he was going to suffer the same fate as Blackwell.

He concentrated on using his feet to help prop him higher and raised his body enough to bend his stomach over the top. But he couldn't get over completely and slid down, leaving him dangling once again.

His pinky was forcibly popped off the edge of the roof.

"What the...?" The wind took the rest of the words from his mouth.

Roy searched the area above him and caught sight of a multitude of dark tapered fingers unhinging his grip. One by one. His right hand was almost completely off, when someone shouted nearby.

"Roy!"

Stomping feet echoed above him.

"Where is he?" Deputy Tran asked.

"I know he's here! I saw him dangling!"

The tiny fingers worked faster, but completely dispersed into a cloud of ash when Kae leaned over the roof and threw herself halfway over to grab a tight hold of his arm.

"Help me!"

Tran was suddenly there, bearing half the weight so each woman gripped an arm hard and dragged him to the right side of the roof.

Roy used the last of his energy reserves to propel himself against their support, until he tumbled over and with their help landed on his feet. If not for his rescuers, he wouldn't be able to stand.

"Are you okay?" Kae was breathing heavily but still gripped him.

He only managed a nod because he was struggling to catch his breath.

"How did you end up hanging from the side of the building, Sir?" Tran asked, stepping away and waiting for his answer.

"I..." Roy gritted his teeth and sucked in shallow breaths because all the muscles in his body ached when he breathed too deeply.

"He needs to go to the ER," Kae said.

"You... saved... my life." His breath came in spurts but his heart swelled. "Both... of... you."

"We did what we had to," she said.

"Thank… you."

Tran lowered her eyes and took another step back. "We should take you to the emergency room, Sir."

He nodded and she walked away.

When Kae was about to help him follow her lead, he tightened his grip on her.

"How… did you… know?"

There was something in her eyes he couldn't read. "I—"

"Sir!"

Roy looked up to find his deputy was waiting by the door.

Kae sighed. "Come on, you need to get checked out."

"I know…" Yet, all he wanted to do was embrace her and never let go.

"I can't believe he was right," she said.

"Who?"

"Steven Blackwell."

7:33pm

"How are you feeling?" Kae's concern echoed across the line. "Are you sure you're going to be okay on your own?"

He wished he was with her.

"Yeah, I'm sure," he said. "What's the worst that can happen?"

"Don't say things like that in this town. Thicket has a way of using words against you."

She was right about that, but didn't want to add to her worry, so he didn't say anything.

"I can't get the image of you hanging over the side of the building out of my head."

"You should, because I survived. Thanks to you."

"And Betty."

"Of course." He knew his deputy was an integral part of him living another day, but Kae was the one who'd alerted her. "How did you know I was there, again?"

"I was already at the hospital."

Roy couldn't forget what she'd told him on the roof. That Steven Blackwell was somehow right. About what? Besides, how could the young man be right about anything when he was dead? He didn't get a chance to ask her exactly what she'd meant because he'd ended up in the ER for a while, answered Betty's questions afterward, and by then Kae was busy signing the release papers for Molly.

"I know you were, but what you said on the roof—"

"Isn't important."

"Kae, you know that's not true." He sighed and rubbed his eyes. "Every detail matters, and if you happen to know something about Steven that might help with the investigation, you have to tell me."

"I don't think this will help."

"Why not?"

"The last time I checked, ghosts couldn't give statements or testify in court."

He sat up and a twinge on the back of his shoulders made him wince.

"What's wrong? Are you okay?"

"Yeah, I'm a bit tender."

"I'm so glad nothing is broken."

"Yeah, me too. But Kae, what the hell does that mean? Are you telling me you saw a ghost?" A chill raced down his spine when Roy recalled what he'd seen inside Molly's hospital room, and the presence on the roof. Not to mention those shadowy fingers trying to pry his hand open on the roof.

"Okay, but it's going to make me sound nuts."

"Just tell me, please. I need to know."

Kae's sigh echoed inside his ears.

"I saw Steven's ghost in my rearview mirror—twice." She paused for two seconds too long. "First, when I arrived at the hospital and he told me to pass on a message to you."

"What was the message?"

"That he didn't jump, he was pushed."

"By who?"

"He didn't say." Kae paused for another second before barreling on. "The second time I saw him was when I was leaving. That's when he told me you were on the roof and in danger. Steven said someone was going to push you, so I ran out of the car and tried calling you but couldn't get through… And by the time I reached the hospital, there you were. Dangling from the side."

"I'm sorry, Kae. I really am." While on speakerphone, he checked his cell and found six missed calls from her. The reception really was a drag in this town. Not that he could've answered.

"Don't be sorry, I'm glad we got there in time." She was clearly crying now and not being by her side to comfort her tore at his heart.

"I'm glad too, and will forever be grateful."

Kae was quiet on her end, but he could hear sniffling so he waited until she was ready to continue. "What happened up there?"

"I don't know," he said, though if she was being honest with him, he owed her the same respect. "I went to the roof to see if I could find any clues and didn't feel like I was alone up there. I swear there was someone—or something—pushing against me, trying to make sure I fell over the side."

"That sounds as weird as what I just told you."

"It sure does." He decided to keep the shadowy fingers that turned to ash to himself. "There's nothing natural about what's going on in Thicket." *Not since Molly came back.* But he couldn't tell her that.

"I wish you were staying the night."

"Me too, but we both decided it wasn't a good idea until Molly settles in."

"I know, I know. It doesn't mean I won't miss you like crazy, though."

"Same here." Roy hated to cut off their conversation, but he knew it was the right thing to do. "Speaking of Molly, I better let you go so you can spend some time with her."

"Yeah... I guess. Anyway, what're you doing?"

"Watching a game."

She scoffed. "What game?"

"Don't know, don't care."

"I love your honesty."

"And I love you, Kaelyn Ventura."

"Love you too, Roy Everly." Her warm laughter filled him with joy. "One of these days I'll get rid of the dreadful Roscoe I've been too lazy to remove and return to my former maiden glory."

"Maybe you've been waiting for a fresh new name all along," he dared to say out loud. This wasn't the first time he'd considered asking Kae to marry him. The first time was the day before she'd left for college. The latest was only last week.

"Maybe I have."

He couldn't help but grin. "I'll call you tomorrow."

"I can't wait."

Roy disconnected and leaned back into his favorite armchair. He grabbed the cool bottle of beer beside him and took a swig. The muted baseball game on TV played on even though he wasn't even sure who the teams were. He wasn't much of a sports fan, but the images provided a background for his wandering mind. Drinking alcohol wasn't the best way to deal with the discomfort on his shoulder, but it beat taking another painkiller.

The pills he'd left on the coffee table under a handful of paperbacks teased him, but he ignored the familiar pull.

He couldn't stop thinking about the creepy shit he'd noticed lately. Ghosts, phantom winds, invisible pressure—none of these compared to the lure of prescription drugs.

His heart ached for Kae because he understood her confusion about Molly. The teenager refused to talk to her mother, and he still couldn't forget what she'd done to Kae in the hospital room. His breath caught. How did a young girl manage to push her mother across the room without so much as touching her? Was this connected to the incident on the roof? If Steven was pushed, and Roy could've sworn he'd seen Molly up there, did she have something to do with this? But the girl was restrained to the hospital bed.

Roy couldn't do much about Kae's familial problems, but he needed to continue his investigation. And that included Molly. The teen's refusal to answer questions, the unexpected death of the police officer guarding her, and then Roy almost ending up the same, had one thing in common—*her*.

"Why won't Molly talk?" He felt silly voicing the question, but this wasn't the first time he'd talked to himself. Living alone encouraged this sort of thing.

A thump made him jolt in his armchair.

The rain might be over, but the wind hadn't calmed yet. Something in the yard had probably smacked into the side of the house.

Roy tried to concentrate on the game.

The second thump was harder, made the window rattle.

He pocketed his cell, dumped the beer on the coffee table and grabbed his gun as he headed for the backdoor. His pulse thundered in his temples as he approached and told himself a hundred different reasons why he shouldn't go out there to check. But he was a police officer—the Sheriff of this town—and hiding wasn't his style.

A third thump bounced off the house.

"Shit." He opened the door and walked out slowly, with the S&W pointed in front of him. He stepped on the dewy grass and checked the side of the house.

There was nothing there, but he could clearly see black streaks under the window.

The thump echoed behind him and he swiveled, gun at the ready, to find—nothing.

His bare feet squelched into the grass when he headed for the backdoor, only to hear the sound coming from the other side of the house.

Roy rushed ahead and slammed into a wall of ice. He bounced off and his breath misted as the yard was blocked from view by a dark wall. An infinity of black stretched out in every direction, paralyzing him to the spot.

His arm dropped to the side and the gun slipped from his numb fingers.

The wall rippled like an oil spill and he couldn't see past it.

He tilted his head and vaguely made out the shape of a head with large antlers—or branches—stretching impossibly high.

Captivating fiery eyes caught his gaze, held him steady until all he wanted to do was surrender.

To give up his soul and the life coursing through his veins.

It wasn't until he heard his son calling him that he was able to break eye contact with those fire-pits. It took every ounce of strength he possessed, but he lowered his head.

"Billy?" What the fuck was in that beer?

"Don't give up, Dad."

"Where are you, son?" Tears blurred his vision and he blinked them away.

"Run, Dad!"

A deafening growl vibrated around him, twisted the oily wall in swirls that swallowed Billy's face.

"No, come back!"

The wall rippled, and he spotted countless other faces. Children, popping in and out of focus. When he saw Molly's face, his heart almost stopped beating.

"What the fuck is happening?"

He caught sight of shadowy tentacles from the corner of his eye. Multiple shadows rushed him, whipped his body so hard he didn't get the chance to escape the smoke creeping in through his eyes and mouth. The crawling sensation filled his throat and esophagus, slipped like thick sludge into his stomach, keeping him pinned to the spot like a helpless bug.

Pain unlike any he'd ever encountered tore him from the inside out.

Roy gritted his teeth when the darkness overwhelmed him.

8:00pm

"Here you go. A hot bowl of chicken soup will make you feel better..." Kae's voice trailed off when she reached her daughter's bedroom. She wasn't where she'd left her, tucked into bed. "Molly?"

A wave of panic tore through her. The tray trembled in her arms, so she took a quick breath because she didn't want to make a mess.

Molly has to be somewhere inside this house.

The front door was locked and the twins were tucked in. She suddenly wished Molly had stayed in the hospital for another day or two—maybe a week. Hell, she'd even toyed with the idea of letting Devin take her to his place.

Kae's heart fell. She had to be the most ungrateful and selfish parent ever. After wishing Molly would come back for so long, now that she was here... all she could do was fantasize about getting rid of her.

"Molly?" Kae walked the length of the hallway and took the stairs as slowly as she could. Worse than spilling the soup would be landing in it. She glanced at the front door, happy to find it was still locked.

She wasn't in the living room, either.

"Molly?" She wandered past the kitchen and into the sunroom. Where the teenager sat in the wicker chair facing the gaping window. "There you are!" She rushed inside. "It's too cold to have this open."

She sat with her knees tucked under her chin, pale arms wrapped around her legs.

"Honey, are you listening to me?" She placed the tray on the table and rushed to shut the window.

Kae shivered against the bitter night air, feeling a sense of wrongness sweep over her as she rubbed her arms.

"Why aren't you in your room?" She couldn't understand why Molly would choose to leave the bedroom she'd once loved so much.

She might have returned physically, but mentally she's still lost in the woods.

"I made some warm soup for you." Kae took her time back to the table and stood in front of Molly with the tray in her arms. "It's your favorite."

Dark circles made the skin under Molly's eyes appear bruised, and the cracks on the corners of her mouth caught saliva bubbles. The stitches peeking out from her pajama top appeared so much darker, she couldn't help but remember the doctor mentioning vines.

"Here, we can put this on your lap and—"

Molly shoved the tray away, toppling the bowl and spoon. Soup splashed all over the floor.

"What the hell did you do that for?" She couldn't stop the anger from surfacing. How could her child be such an ungrateful little bitch?

Molly didn't respond, hadn't moved an inch. And her eyes never strayed from the window. What did she see outside?

Kae sighed as she went about picking up the bowl and tray. The soup was all over the wooden floor and had squirted on some surfaces, but she wasn't in the mood to clean up.

"Don't open the window!"

She didn't even blink.

Kae was about to leave the room when a horrifying scream split the night, causing a shiver to ripple down her spine.

Without thinking, she dumped the bowl and tray and marched into the chilly night.

Another scream made her chest constrict. She doubled over, tried to catch her breath as the most horrendous pain tore through her body. Her hair was damp and stuck to her face. She willed her numb legs to head back inside but as she took the last step, the backdoor slammed in her face.

"No!" She went to the door and tried to open it, but couldn't. Molly was sitting in the same spot, still catatonic. "Shit."

She left the backyard and raced along the side of the house, until she reached the front and found the fake-rock. Her excitement faded when she found the key holder empty. Was the world conspiring against her tonight? That key had stayed hidden since the days when she was married to Devin.

Kae dumped the useless lump and headed for the front door. She tried to open it, but of course it was locked. She'd made sure it was. Maybe she could go to one of the neighbors, but none had a spare key to her house. She had no other option but to knock and hope one of the twins heard her.

After several unsuccessful knocks, Tessa responded.

Kae pushed through the gap and slammed the door.

"Mama, what happened?"

She pushed the hair out of her face. "I got locked out."

"What were you doing outside?"

"I, uh…" What excuse could she tell her youngest daughter that would sound credible? "I had to take out the garbage."

"Oh."

"Get back to bed." She forced a smile on her face, even though all she wanted to do was cry. "I'm sorry I woke you."

"You didn't," she said, yawning.

Her pulse thundered. "Having trouble sleeping again?"

"Uh-huh."

"You didn't go outside, did you?"

"No."

"Were you having another tree monster nightmare?"

Tessa shrugged and she didn't push. "Let's get you back to bed."

She led Tessa into her bedroom, tucked her in and she was asleep as soon as her head hit the pillow. It wasn't until she went to check on Tommy that her pulse sped up because he wasn't in his bed.

Kae practically ran to the sunroom.

Her heart skipped a beat when she spotted the open window. But that wasn't the worst of it. Tommy was facing the window, and appeared to be stuck to the spot as tendrils of darkness writhed in from the night and held his body steady.

"What the hell is happening?" She ran to her son and screamed. The tentacles were holding him up, but the tips were buried deep inside his eye sockets and mouth.

Kae tried to yank the horrid things out, but her hands went through as if she were trying to grab fog. Black residue colored her fingers, reminded her of smoke tinted with ash.

She shut the window so hard, the house rattled.

The darkness vanished into the cold air, releasing her son.

Tommy shook his head and she fell to her knees in front of him, rubbing his arms, trying to get some heat into his cold skin.

"Are you okay?"

"What… what am I doing here?"

"You must have been sleepwalking." She didn't know what else to say. This wasn't something he'd ever done. "Let's get you back to bed."

As Kae encouraged her son out of the sunroom, she glanced at Molly and found her still sitting in the wicker chair.

After tucking Tommy back into bed, she watched from the doorway for several minutes.

She tried calling Roy, but her call went to voicemail. She didn't bother leaving a message and instead sent him a text.

He didn't respond, was probably asleep by now.

Butterflies fluttered in her stomach when she thought about what Roy hinted at during their last call. She'd love to be his wife.

Kae stuck the cellphone in her pocket and headed back to the sunroom. She ignored the mess and stood in front of her daughter.

"What was happening to your brother?"

She blinked once.

"Did you have anything to do with what was happening to him?"

She blinked twice.

"Talk to me!" She slammed her palms against the sides of the chair but Molly didn't react. "Answer me, damn it."

She blinked three times.

"Molly, what's going on?" She was suddenly in the air, flying across the room until she landed awkwardly on the wicker table.

She left the sunroom and sobs caught in her throat. She closed her bedroom door and collapsed on the bed until she couldn't cry anymore.

Kae refused to put the twins in further danger. Not after what happened to Tommy.

She wiped her face, yanked the phone from her pocket and dialed.

"Kaelyn?"

"Yeah, it's me, Devin." She sighed. "I need your help."

"Did something happen?"

She ignored his question. "Can the twins stay with you for a while?"

"Of course, but what's going on?"

"I'll take them to school tomorrow, can you pick them up?"

"Uh, I've got classes all day, but I can get Sofia to pick them up."

"Okay, fine." She wasn't going to argue the specifics.

"Kae, what's wrong?"

I think they're in danger. But she didn't tell him that.

DAY THREE

Thursday
November 12, 2015

7:00am

Devin being Devin, he turned up at the house early in the morning. Even after they'd already made plans, he had to change them. This was another habit of his she couldn't stand but put up with for years. At least he'd be able to get them to school on time.

Kae met him at the front door before he had a chance to knock. "What're you doing here? I thought we discussed—"

"What's the big deal? I've got a day off, so I thought I'd save you the trouble."

"Don't you have classes today?"

"Plans change." He looked her over. "You don't look so good, are you sick? Is that why you want me to take the kids?"

"No, I'm not sick. I didn't get much sleep." After the ordeal in the sunroom, she hadn't been able to relax. She hadn't showered yet, or eaten for hours. The thought of those black tentacles—or whatever those things were—haunted the small amount of slumber she did manage. And if that wasn't enough, Molly refused to eat anything she offered, and she still hadn't been able to get in touch with Roy.

"Well, you look like shit."

"Great, thanks."

"I'm only—"

"You always know how to make a girl feel special."

"You're hardly a girl—"

"Shut the fuck up, you're not baiting me today." She turned away and headed into the house. "I'm not in the mood for your crap and don't have time for your shit."

"Wow, good morning to you too." He turned back and waved before following her inside.

"Are you going to leave her waiting in the car again?" She wasn't stupid, had caught sight of Sofia in the passenger seat.

He closed the door. "Did you get out of the wrong side of the bed?"

She didn't deign him with a response. "I'll get the kids."

"Wait a sec, I want to see Molly first."

"Yeah, okay, maybe you'll get a response from her."

"What'd you mean?"

Kae shrugged. "She hasn't said a word since she got home, refuses to eat, doesn't leave the sunroom and looks worse than before."

"Have you called the hospital?"

"There's a counselor coming over later, so I'll ask her for advice. Otherwise, I'll have to call Dr. Misra and see if she needs to be hospitalized again."

"But she just got out of that place! Surely, you're exaggerating."

"Check for yourself." She motioned for him to go. "I'll get the kids."

"Sure, okay."

Kae left him in the hallway and went to the twin's adjoining rooms separated by their shared bathroom.

She found Tessa staring at her backpack.

"Hey, honey."

"Hi Mama." She considered the book in her hand. "Are you sure I need to take my schoolbag? Aren't we going to stay with Dad and Other Mom for the weekend?"

"It's not the weekend yet." She sighed, hated to do this to the twins. "You need to take your school stuff because I don't know how long you'll be staying."

"Okay." She stuck the book inside and zipped up the backpack. "Is it because of Molly?"

Kae didn't want to lie. "Your sister is really sick and needs special attention. If things get worse, I don't want you kids to have to see…"

"But you will."

"I know, honey, but I'm a grownup and it's kind of my job to deal with things when they don't go well."

"What's wrong with her?"

"I'm not sure," she said, honestly. "We still don't know where she went." She took a breath, hated having this conversation with her younger kids. "Or what she went through."

"Do you think she'll ever remember us?" Her eyes were shiny.

"I hope so."

"She hasn't forgotten everything."

"What do you mean?" Kae's pulse sped up as she sat beside her youngest.

Tessa shrugged.

She took her hand. "Honey, if you know something, you have to tell me. I want to help Molly, but I don't know how."

Tessa sighed before whispering, "She hasn't forgotten Czort."

"The urban myth?"

"Yep."

"When did she remember that?"

"She keeps mumbling it under her breath."

"I haven't heard her mumble anything. She hasn't spoken a word since she got home."

"She won't stop and it hurts my ears. It's why I haven't spent much time with her," she said, and sounded sad. "Tommy doesn't mind because he uses it to scare me all the time."

Kae still remembered the verse from her childhood. Every kid in Thicket did because it was tradition. A disturbing way for parents to scare their kids out of going too deep into the woods. And a very convenient way for kids to terrorize each other.

If you venture into the woods alone,
he'll be waiting for you.
If you look deep into his eyes,
he'll come for you.
If you're brave enough to stay,
he'll never let you go.

It was a silly warning that didn't even rhyme.

"You know that's just a silly story, right? A way for people to scare themselves and others?" She wrapped an arm around Tessa's shoulders. "It's not real."

"I know it's supposed to be a story, but then Molly went missing in the woods and now that she's back she looks like a zombie."

"She's not a zombie, she's still your sister."

"She doesn't *feel* like my sister." Tessa shook her head. "I don't see Molly when I look into her eyes. I see other *things* looking back at me. Maybe it's the souls that surrender to Czort."

"I don't remember anything about that."

"It's in the second part," she said. "Besides, all myths and legends come from something real, superstition."

"Who told you that?"

"Other Mother loves folklore and fairy tales and she tells the best ones. Ones that are creepy and dark, not like the Disney versions."

The thought of another woman teaching her kids anything she didn't know about concerned her. These were *her* kids, and a twenty-something who'd wandered into their lives a handful of years ago had no business teaching them anything. She swallowed the anger and jealousy, because this unexpected conversation involved Molly's condition.

"What else did she tell you?"

"That Czort is called the Black One. He hunts and lures kids into the woods with his red eyes and swallows their willing souls."

"That doesn't sound like good bedtime reading to me." She'd have to talk to Devin about this, or maybe Sofia herself. No wonder Tessa had been having more nightmares than usual.

"It's not," she said with a nod. "She tells me this in her office, where she keeps all her books and papers."

"Oh, okay." Good to see her college education had paved the way for something more than finding a husband in her professor.

"That's why Molly scares me."

"Honey, I don't want you to worry, okay? You're going to spend some time with Dad and Oth— Sofia, so I don't want you to worry about your sister. I'll be here with her, to make sure she recovers. Hopefully, by the time you come back, she'll be better."

"I'll try, and will ask Other Mother what she thinks."

She was about to object, but decided to keep quiet. At this stage, any insight could come in handy. "Let me know if you find out anything useful. Now, finish packing."

Tessa hopped off the bed. "Hypnosis might be an option."

"What?"

"If someone forgets what happened to them and they get hypnotized, it helps them remember."

"Is this something else Sofia told you about?"

"Other Mother even lent me a book about it. It's really interesting."

"She shouldn't be showing you things like that." And why hadn't she noticed her twelve-year-old daughter reading a book about hypnosis? *Probably because she reads it when you're not around.*

It wasn't fair for the kids to get caught in the middle of the problems adults had caused. She knew the twins felt guilty about enjoying their time at Devin's house, and a lot of that was because they loved Sofia. She was attentive and treated them as if they were her own. Sometimes that really got under her skin, made her blood boil. But now, while taking a step back and looking at the scene objectively, she could see how unfair she made things sometimes.

"Other Mother's been studying this all of her life. Her mother passed the knowledge on to her and she's going to teach me what she knows." Her eyes lit up. "Maybe while I'm staying with them, she can teach me something to help Molly."

"Maybe." Though this was a lie because she didn't want anyone teaching her kids such weird mumbo-jumbo.

"I want to help."

"Are you all packed up?"

"Yep."

"What about your brother?"

"He must still be in his room."

She stood, feeling tiredness sweep through her. "Get all your stuff together and leave it near the front door."

"Okay."

She walked into her son's room. "Hey, Tommy..." He wasn't in there and neither were his bags.

Kae's heart was beating too fast as she entered the sunroom to find Devin sitting across from Molly. His eyes were glazed. Tommy stood in front of the window again.

"Get away from there!"

He didn't budge.

"Thomas!"

"Huh?" He swung around to face her and as he did, the glaze faded from his eyes.

"Get your stuff and take it to the front door."

"Uh, yeah, sure."

"And don't forget your school things!"

With him gone, she dared to cross the room. When she reached her ex-husband's side, he seemed to be in a trance.

She slapped his shoulder. "The kids are ready."

"Ow!" Devin pretended to be hurt.

"Don't be such a baby, I didn't hit you that hard." She sighed. "What were you doing, anyway?"

"Talking to..."

"You weren't talking to anyone."

"I was speaking to our daughter."

"So, she spoke to you?"

"Sure did."

"What did she say?"

"You know, I don't remember." He rubbed the stubble on his jaw. "But you were right, she's not looking very healthy. Maybe she needs a bit of sun. Taking her into the yard might be a good place to start."

"Thanks for the advice, *Doctor.*"

Devin kissed the top of Molly's head as he stood. "I'll come back to see you soon."

Not if she could help it. Right now, the best thing for Devin to do was to take the younger kids across town and not come back until whatever the fuck was going on sorted itself out. *Or rather, I sort it out.* Because it was becoming very obvious that the time to be passive was over. She had to get proactive.

"Bye Daddy," Molly whispered.

She couldn't believe it. These were the first words she'd spoken since getting home. Well, the only ones she'd heard. According to Tessa, Molly mumbled all the time.

"Bye Baby." He gave Kae a pointed look as they left the sunroom and headed for the front door.

"Hey Dad," Tessa said with a grin.

"Yeah, hi, Dad," Tommy added.

"Weren't you with him in the sunroom?" she asked, confused.

"When?"

"Just now—"

"Kaelyn, I think you need to get some sleep. You're imagining things," Devin said, his voice serious. "How am I supposed to trust you to look after Molly if you're like this? You look like a shambling zombie."

"I'm fine."

"You're not fine," he said, dragging her away from the twins. "I can see your hands are shaking from here. If you don't get some rest, I'll have to come back for Molly as well."

"No!"

"Then take care of yourself." Devin pressed both hands against her shoulders and looked her in the eye. "She's not a baby. Surely you can leave her alone to take a shower." He leaned closer. "Because you're starting to stink."

She tried to shrug him off, but he doubled down.

"I'm serious, chill and get cleaned up. Take a bath, or a nap. Whatever it takes to get you back to the land of the living."

His comment roused a shiver up her spine. "Okay, okay."

"Good. I know how much this has taken out of you. But she's back now, things can only get better."

She doubted that very much but kept her mouth shut. She pulled out of his grabby hands and ruffled Tommy's hair before giving him a one-armed hug. "Take care of your sister and behave."

"I always do," he said with a toothy grin.

Next, she hugged Tessa and whispered, "Make sure you take care of him, okay?"

"I will," she said with a conspiring smile.

As Kae watched her kids make their way down the path and climb into their father's car with bags in tow, she felt a weight slipping from her shoulders. She didn't even mind when she heard them squealing and hugging Sofia, who had waited in the car all this time.

She stood in the doorway, not daring to step outside fully, and waved them away until they were out of sight.

She was going to miss them, but this was the best thing to do—the only thing. She'd already caught Tommy acting strange twice, and the way she'd found Devin chilled her to the bone. If her son couldn't remember standing in the sunroom like a statue only minutes ago, her ex-husband was convinced he'd had a conversation with Molly and neither one recalled being in the same room, there was definitely a problem.

She didn't understand why she was the only one who could see all of this.

Kae was already dialing Roy's number when she entered the house and considered telling Molly she was going to take a shower. She didn't bother and instead flicked the switch on the coffee machine as she listened to his recorded message.

"Hi, you've reached Roy. Please leave a message and your number, if you want me to call you back."

"Roy, it's me. I've left you a hundred messages already, so I'm starting to tread into stalker territory, but please, call me back." She sighed. "I'm really worried about you."

Time Unknown

Roy heard a familiar tinkling coming from somewhere, but didn't know what it was.

On some level, he recognized the sound but couldn't place it.

He was safely cocooned inside the most comfortable shelter. As long as he remained calm, he would always feel at peace.

Yet something kept scratching at the back of his mind. Why was he surrounded by total darkness? Hadn't morning come yet? Shouldn't he be getting ready for work? Work. What was work? Somewhere he went, something he *had* to do.

A duty he shouldn't ignore because he was in the middle of an investigation—Molly, Steven, the roof, they were all connected somehow.

"I have to go to work."

He owed it to Steven, the young deputy who'd lost his life when he was pushed over the roof. He owed it to Molly, the young girl who didn't speak to anyone because she was traumatized. And he owed it to Kae. Kaelyn needed him. Now more than ever.

"I need to wake up."

You are *awake.*

Roy sat up and his eyes were already opened, but he didn't recognize his surroundings. He wasn't in his backyard. He should be there. That's where he'd ended up after something smacked into the side of his house.

He reached for his gun, but it wasn't there.

The tinkling sound came again, followed by a beep.

"Is that... is that my phone?" He could feel it, tucked into his back pocket, unreachable because his limbs refused to work. "Where am I?"

You're home.

"This isn't home." Home was with Kae.

He stared at the thick branches overhead as the leaves rustled in the wind that didn't reach him. Caught sight of another overcast day peeking through the thick canopy, and the glare hurt his eyes.

Roy could see, but couldn't feel.

Sudden excruciating pain tore him apart, snapped his bones and stretched his skin. Curved his spine until he was bent backwards and staring at an upside-down world without a sky.

4:00pm

"What the hell are you doing?" Kae yanked the steaming coffee pot from Molly's quivering hands. Brown droplets dribbled down her chin, stained the front of her pajamas and her lips bubbled with blisters. "Why did you do that?"

Kae left her alone for fifteen minutes and her teenage daughter had poured boiling coffee into her mouth. She shouldn't have started the machine before the shower, but had anticipated having a nice cup of coffee while they waited for the counselor to arrive.

Wasn't she allowed a moment of peace?

Molly was worse than a toddler.

"What were you thinking?"

She didn't say a word, stood like a zombie.

Kae soaked a washcloth in cold water and wiped her chin and chest. Molly's eyes were unfocused but she winced.

"Did you hurt yourself on purpose? If you want coffee, I can make you some."

Molly dipped her head in the smallest of nods.

"Sit down over here." She ushered Molly to the breakfast nook and she collapsed onto the seat. "Wait here and I'll get you a cup."

It didn't take long to get another pot brewed, so she filled the biggest mug she could find all the way to the top. "Here you go." She placed it in front of Molly and even added a plate of leftover choc-chip cookies.

As soon as the counselor arrived, she planned to duck out to check on Roy. He didn't live far, and she'd be back with plenty of time to get an update on Molly's condition. For now, she stood at the kitchen counter and watched as her once-capable daughter fumbled with the mug as she drank the contents without pause. She refilled the cup two more times. This wasn't nutritious, but at least she was consuming *something.*

She ducked into the bathroom, came back with a tube of aloe vera and squeezed a generous amount on her fingertips. "Let me apply this to your chin so it soothes the burn."

Molly pulled her head back, almost hitting the wall.

"Let me help you," she insisted.

She struggled against her, but Kae wasn't going to back down.

"I want to help my daughter, is that so bad?" She managed to hold her still and dabbed a generous amount of aloe on Molly's chin. She cried out, loud shrills of pain that made her skin smoke. "What's wrong?"

Before she could do anything else, that now familiar pressure she'd encountered several times shoved against her shoulders and pushed her to the floor. The back of her head hit the tiles, caused her vision to fade out for a second.

She tried to get up but something was keeping her shoulders pinned.

When she looked up, Molly stood over her. Her eyes were hollow pits of despair sending Kae's mind into a tailspin. Her skin prickled when she spied a familiar face lost in the darkness within.

"Roy..."

A knock on the door roused her.

Molly was still at the nook, as if she'd never moved at all.

She scrambled to her feet, rubbed the back of her head, and shambled down the corridor to answer the door.

"Good afternoon, my name's Emilia Irwin and I'm the counselor who's been assigned to Molly." The short, plump blonde woman pushed her glasses further up her nose and held out her right hand.

"Oh, yeah, hi. I'm Kaelyn Roscoe." She shook the offered hand. "Come in, Molly's in the kitchen." But when they reached the nook, she wasn't there. "She must've gone into the sunroom. It's where she spends most of her time. She refuses to stay in her bedroom."

"I see." She followed close behind, surveying her surroundings.

As expected, there she was, motionless, back in the wicker chair facing the window.

"She won't stop looking out that window."

The counselor nodded. "She's picked something to focus on, to keep her grounded."

"Is that normal?"

"Is anything she's been through normal?" Emilia's voice was soft and soothing, with a melodic tang she hoped would comfort Molly.

"We still don't know what happened."

"And you may never know." Emilia placed a comforting hand on Kae's arm and met her eyes. "Abductions are hard on the person who was taken, but have a domino effect. That she doesn't remember could be true, or it might be that she doesn't want to talk about her experience. Either way, she's bound to cause unintentional pain. While you want her to be the same person she used to be, she'll probably never be the child you lost."

"It's... she doesn't talk to me."

"Sometimes, when someone struggles to say what they really want, they can reveal what they mean without words."

She sighed. "I'm at my wit's end. All I want is for my daughter to speak to me."

"I understand." Emilia's smile was sympathetic, sad. She approached Molly and left her bag on the wicker table.

At least Kae had righted the mess and cleaned up the soup spill from the night before.

"What happened to her face?"

"I took a quick shower and when I came downstairs, I found her in the kitchen drinking straight from the coffee pot."

"Oh goodness, her skin is inflamed." Her brow furrowed as she examined her, keeping a safe distance.

"I tried to apply some aloe vera, but she pushed me away."

"So, she's reckless *and* skittish."

"Is that normal?"

"I wouldn't say that exactly, but it's definitely character traits I've seen before from someone suffering PTSD."

Kae wasn't going to get anywhere if this woman had an answer to soften out every groove with some sort of theory. "Is it okay if I leave you with her for a bit?"

Emilia nodded. "That's fine, and might even be beneficial. If you give her some space, she might talk to me. Sometimes a stranger is easier to confide in than a parent."

"I won't be long." She pretended the words didn't wound her as much as all the other negativity Molly had brought into her life since returning. She stifled the wave of anger and resentment before it flared up.

"Take as long as you need, I won't leave until you get back."

"Thank you."

"Good afternoon, Molly," the counselor said, moving towards the teen in the same way one would approach a wild animal. "My name is Emilia and I'm here to listen to anything you want to say. Anything at all." She flashed Kae a dismissive smile and motioned for her to go.

Kae took the hint and left the sunroom, glad to dump this burden on someone else for a while.

She tried to call Roy but he didn't answer, so she dialed the Sheriff's department.

5:00pm

Kae parked on the road in front of Roy's house and switched off the engine.

She sat in the car and surveyed the area. His cruiser was parked in the driveway, and so was a second cop vehicle. She could only assume this was Betty's, since she'd spoken to her before leaving the house, and the deputy said she'd check up on him.

Kae grabbed her phone and stepped out of the car. After pocketing her keys, she walked across the grass and glanced at the haphazardly parked car as she passed. The engine was still running and the radio crackled inside, but there was no sign of Betty.

She quickened her step and knocked on the front door.

No answer.

"Roy, are you in there?"

She couldn't hear anyone moving around inside, which didn't sound right if a fellow deputy had come to check he was all right. She knocked a second time but when no one responded, she headed for the side of the house and into the backyard.

"Roy!"

A chill raced through her when she stared at the tree line at the end of the yard.

"Betty!"

The squeaky hinges of the open backdoor made her gasp. Why was it swinging in the breeze?

"Roy! Betty!" She ran into the house. "Where are you?"

He wasn't in the kitchen, neither was Betty. Weak light streamed in through the two windows, and she noticed a few cups and a plate in the sink. Nothing else seemed to be out of place because Roy kept a tidy house.

"Roy?"

Kae strolled into the gloomy hallway and paused to look at the single photo frame hanging on one side of the wall. Billy's last school photo showed a vibrant young boy with the same crooked smile as his father. His brown eyes were shiny and he seemed so happy.

Billy Everly would forever be this cheerful twelve-year-old. He never got older, never had the chance to live his own life. Every time his father saw this photo, he would realize the horror of that all over again.

Tears rolled down her face because she was truly a horrible parent. Her missing child *did* come back, but all Kae wanted to do was put distance between them. She constantly felt sorry for herself because Molly didn't behave the same way as the teenage girl who'd left for a jog early one morning and didn't return.

She wiped her eyes and turned away from the photo. Away from everything this frame symbolized, and headed deeper into the gloom.

"Roy, are you okay?"

The living room was also vacant, though the muted TV was on. A bottle of beer sat half-full on the coffee table.

After checking the bathroom and two bedrooms, she decided something weird was definitely going on. How did someone simply vanish into thin air? The thought made her heart sink because that's exactly what had happened to Molly. One day she was there, all smiles and attitude, ready to enjoy a nice summer, the next she was gone. Had the same thing happened to Roy? She couldn't handle going through this all over again.

There you go again—me, me, me!

She pushed away the pesky inner voice and tried to think rationally. Maybe Roy had ducked out for a walk, or decided to stop by the grocery store. But he was injured, so why wouldn't he take the cruiser? And where the hell was Betty?

"Deputy Tran, are you in here?"

When the only response she received was eerie silence, she shivered.

Being a real estate agent had given her a sixth sense about places. The undeniable coziness of lived-in houses—even apartments—was an ambiance she felt as soon as she entered. The light was always warmer, inviting. Even after the residents had moved out, their time in that space left behind a pleasant residue. Empty houses were nothing more than hollowed-out shells because time had stolen all the warmth, leaving behind an abandoned husk. That was the vibe Roy's house was emanating, and it was all wrong.

Kae left through the backdoor and walked across the muddy grass with her eyes focused on the dense trees. She could almost feel something calling to her, watching as she neared.

Someone was waiting.

"Roy, are you out there?" Her voice echoed through the dense vegetation, but he didn't reply. "Betty, is that you?"

Kae's breath caught in her throat as frustration and fear warred with each other.

"Where are you?" Her anguished yell startled the birds and a multitude took flight, shedding feathers and cracking branches in their wake.

Kae's heart was pounding too fast, and a sense of total and utter wrongness made her skin goose pimple. The closer she got to the tree line, the murkier the woods seemed to become and stretched out impossibly far.

A presence shifted within and she hoped it was Roy, who'd been out for a walk after all. She didn't understand what was happening until she spotted two shiny orange spots, high in the branches. As she stood there, dumbfounded, the dots sunk lower until they were at eye level, and she could clearly see the hollows were filled with flames.

Her skin crawled and every hair on her body stood on end.

"Roy…"

Kae stood her ground and dared to face the approaching darkness and those uncanny fiery eyes.

A black tentacle of smoke whipped out from the trees and wrapped itself around her forearm. The grip was as firm as a blood pressure cuff, but cut her circulation completely. She struggled to pull out of the punishing grasp by raising her arm and when a beam of sunlight touched the smoky limb, the ash dissipated.

Her breath was coming too fast when the fabric of her sweater burned away and left a rosy imprint on her skin.

"ROY!" she screamed until her throat was raw.

Until the darkness spread in front of her to reveal some sort of twisted monster that was quickly replaced by smoky wandering limbs.

"Please, Roy, don't leave me," she whispered before running away. Only to falter when she ended up on her hands and knees. She'd tripped over his gun. Why was his weapon here, lost in the grass?

Kae hesitated. Her spine bent when the tentacle whipped her back. Ash flew all around her as she struggled to her feet, finding it hard to get her footing because of the unstable mud. But she somehow managed to run before she was recaptured.

She raced for her car, slid into the driver's seat and locked the door. Her hands trembled so much it took several tries to put the key into the ignition, but once the engine was running, she took off without a second look.

When she glanced in the rearview mirror, she half-expected to find Roy there.

Time Unknown

"Roy, are you out there?"

The words tore him up inside because he recognized the voice of the first and last woman he'd ever loved. But didn't know where she was or why she was here.

Wherever here was…

This was where he'd seen his son's face and heard his warning, but was too slow to react.

"Roy…"

Although he desperately wanted to see her, he also needed to tell her to go—to leave this place and run as fast as she could. To never look back so she wouldn't end up like him.

His spine curved an inch lower, and the only true sensation left at his disposal was pain.

"ROY!"

"Kae…" Where was she?

A patch of darkness cleared in front of him to reveal an upside-down view of the world. He blinked several times, hoping this would turn his sight the right way up but it didn't. His heart stuttered.

There she was, Kae. Walking on the grass ceiling and calling out his name over and over again. She sounded so far away.

"Kaelyn," he whispered.

"Please, Roy, don't leave me."

He tried to respond but she'd already turned away and was running the other way. What spooked her to make her run like that?

A rush of pain tore through his body when his torso twisted sideways and every bone crackled. His muscles were pulled so tightly, he was sure every single one would snap as easily as his tendons.

"I'll never leave you," he said.

Roy was sucked into an abyss of never-ending agony.

6:00pm

Something terrible had happened at Roy's house, but she couldn't bring herself to call the Sheriff's department because she didn't want anyone else to get hurt. That Betty's car was there and she wasn't, only confirmed how dangerous the situation was.

Kae checked the hole on her sleeve and the stinging skin. What the hell *was* that? She didn't want to make the connection, but already knew it was the same *thing* she'd found lodged inside Tommy's eyes and mouth.

She parked in the driveway and wiped her eyes while staring at the house. The lights were on inside and she hoped the counselor wasn't angry with her. She hadn't meant to take longer than an hour and hadn't bothered to ask how long the visit was meant to last. But Emilia's small blue car was still parked on the street.

As soon as she stepped out, the silence struck her. She looked up and down the street, noticing the sense of isolation creeping in around her. The houses closest to hers were dark, it was only farther down the street that lights glowed from within.

She hated how much this reminded her of the eerie silence in Roy's house.

Her heart sank all over again. What happened to him? Had the smoky tentacles attacked and hauled him into the woods? She regretted not being strong enough to cross the tree line, but how could she when that tentacle threatened to drag her into darkness?

Besides, you have to think about your children. Something she hadn't been doing lately.

Kae rushed up the path and was about to put the key in the lock when the front door opened in front of her. She swallowed and entered the house, ignoring the ice sinking into her lungs.

"Emilia?"

She passed the living room and kitchen, continued into the sunroom.

The ripe stench of body odor assaulted her instantly. She covered her nose, trying to breathe without inhaling the disgusting smell. The counselor was nowhere in sight, but Molly sat in the wicker chair in front of the window.

"Where's the counselor?"

Molly's eyes were cloudy and she was so pale, Kae could see the veins beneath her papery skin. The blistered mess under her mouth was filled with green pus that dribbled down her chin.

"Molly, where's Emilia?" Kae checked the entire house, hoping to find the woman in one of the bathrooms, but she was gone.

As gone as Roy and Betty.

She ignored her treacherous thoughts and returned to the sunroom. Where Emilia's bag sat in the same place.

Kae stopped in front of Molly. "What happened to the counselor?"

Molly sat motionless, with her right shoulder slumped low and her eyes unfocused. She didn't blink, her skin was turning a greenish tinge and she stunk.

"You should take a bath."

Nothing.

"Maybe a shower, then."

Still nothing. Molly didn't bother to raise her head, which drooped to the side as if she found the mass too heavy. More strands were missing from her scalp and Kae nearly threw up when she spotted clumps of hair on her lap.

"I wish you'd talk to me." She watched her for so long, she didn't know if minutes or hours had ticked by. Mother and daughter occupied the same room but were worlds apart. She wanted desperately to understand what happened to Molly while she was gone, but couldn't make her talk.

She wished the compulsion to slap her would surface, but Kae was so defeated she didn't have the energy. All she wanted was for Molly to speak—to say something that wasn't hateful. Hell, at least in the hospital her venomous words were a means of communication. She looked like a dead doll now.

"Please, talk to me." Kae leaned closer, staring into Molly's vacant eyes and hoped she could read some sort of emotion. Instead, she found herself glaring into what resembled a gathering storm of shifting clouds, or was that… smoke? And in between all that smoke she could see a multitude of small, monstrous faces staring back at her.

"What the fuck?" She tried to stand—to leave this room, house, the town if she had to—but couldn't move.

The smoke cleared completely, leaving in its wake the dark hollowed eyes she'd first encountered in the hospital. And inside all this blackness, the faces multiplied. A crowd of *monsters*—because these weren't human faces—were living inside her. And every single one of those distorted figures was drawing her in, until she thought she might fall into Molly's eyes and join them.

Tiny, long fingertips poked out from Molly's left eye, curving over the lower lash line. Another set joined the first, jutting around for a grip.

"No!"

Too many black digits squirmed around the edges of her eye socket like searching spider legs.

The terror of what she saw dragged Kae away from the compelling sensation and she stood too fast, fell.

Kae crawled away from the many fingers trying to escape her daughter's eyes. When she finally managed to get to her feet, she ran. Raced up the stairs and locked herself in the bedroom. Hers was the only one with a lock because a single mother of three sometimes needed uninterrupted time to herself. She never thought she'd need to use it to keep her safe from one of those kids.

Her breath was coming too fast and nausea washed over her while her heart beat like an unstoppable drum. She couldn't believe what was happening.

She made it to the toilet in time to throw up what little she'd managed to eat while trying to deal with this confusing mess. Her skin was sweaty but she was cold, so she sank to the tiles and pressed her face against the wall.

A ding from her pocket made her jump.

Kae dislodged the cellphone from her pocket, hoping what she'd witnessed this afternoon was a horrid nightmare and this was Roy texting her back.

Her heart fell when she found it was a text from Dr. Misra, time stamped three hours ago. *Damn the shitty cell reception in this town.*

Can you come to see me tomorrow morning?

That was all she said, but Kae would definitely go.

The phone rang in her hand and she nearly fainted from the shock.

"Devin."

"Are you okay, Mama?"

"Teresa?" Her heart raced at the sound of her child.

"Yeah, it's me. I wanted to make sure you were okay." She lowered her voice. "I had a nightmare and I was worried about you."

"I'm okay, honey." The lie was necessary because the last thing she wanted was for anyone else to come anywhere near this house.

"Good, I'm glad." Her sigh was too loud. "I love you, Mama."

"Love you too." She let the silent tears roll down her face. "How's your brother? He's not acting weird, is he?"

"Nah, he's as annoying as ever."

Kae laughed because this kind of normalcy felt good amongst all the weirdness.

"I better go, Sofia's making hot chocolate."

She wanted to be doing this with the twins and not someone else, but at least they were being taken care of.

"Tessa, wait!"

"Yeah?"

"Why didn't you call using your phone?"

"It wasn't in my bag. I was sure I packed it, but it wasn't there and Tommy couldn't find his either."

"Oh, I'll check to see if they're in your rooms."

"Thanks."

"Good night, Tessa."

Kae leaned her head against the wall and stayed there until she eventually succumbed to sleep.

DAY FOUR

Friday
November 13, 2015

9:00am

The next morning, Kae's body was stiff after an uncomfortable night caught between the toilet and the sink. She groaned as her muscles protested when she stood, but automatically went about washing her face, brushing her teeth and hair. Applied deodorant to convince herself she could mask the sweat she'd accumulated after last night's ordeal, and was ready to go.

She didn't waste time showering or changing into clean clothes. As long as she looked presentable enough to go to the hospital, that was all that mattered. She couldn't spend another minute inside this house.

She took a breath, left the bathroom, and dared to unlock the bedroom door.

Kae waited with baited breath for smoky tentacles or tiny hands to grab her, but found the corridor empty. The sun was already high and shed sunlight from the window above the staircase.

She took the stairs as fast as she could and didn't bother checking the sunroom. She grabbed her handbag and was out the door in seconds, with keys in hand.

Kae closed the door as quietly as she could and locked it. She turned around and her heart nearly stopped when she found Sienna and Mew standing at the bottom of the porch.

"Good morning, Mrs. Roscoe," Sienna said.

Mew offered his usual shy smile and wave.

"Kids, you scared the hell out of me." She placed a hand on her chest. "What're you doing here? Shouldn't you be at school?"

"Yeah, but we wanted to check on Molly first." Sienna was all smiles, but the cheer didn't reach her eyes.

"That's really nice of you, but she's not feeling very well—"

"What's wrong with her?" Mew asked.

"She needs plenty of rest and is actually asleep right now."

Sienna shook her head, obviously appalled. "You're leaving her on her own?"

"No, there's a counselor with her." She pointed vaguely at the blue car, that had obviously remained parked outside the house overnight. "And I have to duck out for a sec."

The teenagers exchanged a look.

"Okay, we'll come back later," Mew said.

"I really appreciate that." She didn't leave the porch until the two were well on their way and turned the corner.

Kae rushed to her car and drove away faster than she ever had before. She didn't breathe until she reached the intersection, and gripped the steering wheel tightly to stay focused.

St. Jude's Hospital wasn't far from the house, but she still drove like a bundle of nerves with trembling hands and rapid pulse. This was the same way she'd driven the other day, when Roy left a message to tell her they'd found Molly. Back when life was a lot simpler, before she'd found her eldest behaving like a changeling. When the twins were safe at home and Roy hadn't almost fallen off the side of a building, only to vanish the next day. Before she'd seen a ghost in the mirror.

Kae parked as close to the entrance as she could and unbuckled her seatbelt. She wiped the tears from her face and checked to make sure her ghostly passenger hadn't returned. No, she was totally alone.

She blew her nose and waited a few minutes to make sure no one could tell she'd been crying.

She shouldered her bag, climbed out of the car and charged across the parking lot, determined to pretend life was normal for the sake of the kind doctor. She toyed with the idea of actually stopping by the Sheriff's office after, to report what she suspected but wasn't sure if she wanted anyone else involved. Then again, the fact Betty didn't return to the station after a routine check probably alarmed them. In that case, maybe she could stop what was left of the department from ending up the same way.

The automatic doors swished open and she headed straight for the elevators but stopped when she almost smacked into Anthony Benenati. His olive skin was drab and he clearly hadn't shaved in days.

"Anthony," she said.

He looked up, as if he hadn't noticed her even though they'd almost collided. "Hey, Kaelyn, how are you?"

"I'm okay, how are you?"

He shrugged and rubbed his chin.

"How's Allison?"

"She's still in the ICU, hasn't woken from the coma."

Kae wanted to ask if the doctors suspected she never would, but kept her mouth shut. Instead, she sighed and put her hand on his forearm. "I'm so sorry."

"You should go and see her," Anthony said. "She would like that."

"That's a good idea." And she was ashamed she hadn't thought to do this herself, because if Molly was in the car with Allison and she wasn't the one who took her, the only other thing she could've been doing was helping. Maybe she'd found Molly on the side of the road and gave her a ride. "I will."

"How's your daughter?"

"She's… as okay as can be expected."

"I hope she recovers well. At least she's back home in familiar surroundings."

Kae forced a tight-lipped smile and nodded.

"I have to get to work or I'm going to lose my mind," he said. "It was nice to see you."

"Same here. Take care!" Kae watched him go. A man who was usually so perky he put everyone else to shame.

She ducked into the gift store and bought a bouquet of daisies—Allison's favorites.

Kae took the elevator to the sixth floor and headed for Dr. Misra's office, but had to return to the reception desk when she found the office empty.

A harried receptionist was on the phone. When she hung up, she said, "Can I help you?"

"Yeah, hi. I need to see Dr. Misra, but she's not in her office."

"Oh." She consulted the monitor while typing. "Dr. Misra called in sick today."

"She did?"

"Yes."

"But I received a text from her yesterday and was supposed to meet her..."

"I'm sorry, but she's not here."

"Okay." Like everything else in her life at the moment, this didn't make any sense. "What about Emilia Irwin, she's on this floor too, right?"

"She's not in either, I'm afraid."

"Sick as well?"

The receptionist shook her head. "She didn't come in this morning and as far as I know, hasn't called yet."

Kae thanked the woman and was about to walk away when she remembered she was now here for another reason "Where's the ICU?"

"That's a floor above. Why?"

Kae raised the flowers. "I'd like to see Allison Benenati. She's a dear friend of mine and I haven't been in to see her yet."

"I don't know if they'll allow any visitors other than immediate family..."

"I'll check. Thanks for your help."

By the time she reached the next level, she was a bundle of nerves. Dr. Misra had sent her a text that took hours to reach her, and now she wasn't in. Not to mention Emilia, whose car was still parked outside her house. She was running out of excuses to avoid more police involvement.

She left the elevator and the fluorescent lights crackled in a way that reminded her of insects. She swallowed the discomfort, held on tighter to the flowers and continued to the empty reception area.

"Hello?" Kae bit her lip. Should she wait until someone turned up? Or should she sneak in? She was well aware about the restrictions on this floor, so why not take a chance before anyone spotted her?

Kae wandered into the corridor to her right and glanced at the windowed rooms, where machines kept people alive. She passed by a few motionless patients hooked up to ventilators and drips, machines showing heartbeats as shiny, squiggly lines.

She hated doing this because she was an intruder but wouldn't stay for long. Only wanted to leave the daisies for Allison.

Kae found her in the fourth room, where her neighbor lay in bed with machines connected to her. Allison's pale face remained emotionless with too many attachments, and both eyes were closed.

She stopped in front of the window, now wondering if it was a bad idea to step into the room at all. She didn't want to spread germs that shouldn't come in contact with someone in intensive care. Not when Allison was in this situation because of her daughter.

And how did they end up in a car accident? After everything, she had no doubt Molly was somehow responsible for this.

"I'm so sorry," she whispered.

Kae laid the bouquet on the window sill in front of her friend's room and was about to leave, when her neighbor's reflection appeared in the glass. "Oh my God!" She glanced back into the room and found Allison's unconscious body still lying motionless.

"Thanks for the flowers," Allison said with a smile. "They're my favorite."

Kae looked over her shoulder, but she was alone in this hospital corridor.

"If you look away, you won't be able to see or hear me."

"How can you be here *and* there?"

Allison's flimsy reflection shrugged. "I'm slipping away."

"You're dying?"

"Pretty sure I am."

"I'm so sorry, Allison." She swallowed the sadness.

"It's not your fault."

She hoped her next question wasn't as insensitive. "What happened that day?"

Allison's face was almost translucent. "I was driving to work and saw Molly stumbling by the side of the road. I couldn't believe it was her. She looked confused and wouldn't talk, but I coaxed her into the car and headed for the hospital." She sighed. "Just before we got here, I turned to make sure she was okay and the next thing I knew, we'd smashed into a parked car I didn't even see." Allison's reflection flickered. "Gosh, I've been wanting to tell this story for so long, but it's hard when you're unconscious and all."

"Why can I see you, then?" Kae tried not to think about the cause of the accident, because if she'd caught Molly's eye…

"I'm not sure, but something's happening. Something feels different. I've appeared to Anthony and the kids, to the doctors and nurses, but none of them can see or hear me." She looked sad when she added, "No one knows I'm here."

"I know. Though I can probably see you because I'm losing my mind." What other explanation could there be for seeing not one, but two ghosts?

"You're losing a lot of other things, but not your mind."

"What does that mean?"

Allison's rueful smile made her dim. "Being in this state means I can hear things others can't. And I can hear him getting closer."

"Who?"

She flickered like an image caught on film.

"Allison!" But she didn't respond because she was gone.

Kae smacked the window with her fists but knew her friend would never come back.

Allison's heart machine flatlined and several others beeped so loudly, she thought her brain was going to explode.

Nurses and doctors rushed past her.

"You shouldn't be here," one of them said.

"I…"

"Please, you have to leave." The nurse hurried into the small room to join all the other health staff trying to save Allison.

It's too late.

Kae left the ICU in a haze of confusion and fear, too much fear. By the time she reached the lobby she wanted to call Roy, but she couldn't because he wouldn't answer. And neither would Betty. Should she go straight to the Sheriff's department? What could they do against a supernatural entity? She couldn't deny it any longer, she was dealing with something really dark. Something she didn't understand and needed someone like the Warrens to help, or some other paranormal investigator.

A paranormal investigator…

Tessa had mentioned several times that Sofia was into this sort of thing. Even told her the woman claimed to have learned about all types of freaky stuff from her own mother.

As much as she wanted to keep Devin and his wife out of this, the reality was she wouldn't be able to hold them off forever. And if there was even the slightest chance Sofia could help…

It's worth a try.

11:00am

"That's quite a story."

Kae sighed. "I know how it sounds, but I'm telling you the truth."

"I didn't say I don't believe you. You have no idea what kind of things I've seen." Sofia shook her head, as if trying to forget. "My childhood was full of unbelievably dark shit I wouldn't wish on anyone."

Kae sat back in the chair and considered the woman sitting across the kitchen table. She was attractive with lovely green eyes, pouty lips and a shock of wavy red hair. She was slim but curvy, had such a nice figure that skinny jeans and a sweater actually looked stylish on her. And she'd just spilled the insanity of the last few days to someone she barely knew.

When she found her voice again, she said, "Where did you grow up?"

"Originally, I was born in Northern Spain. My father was a former Catholic priest and my mother a former nun. Yeah, I know. It sounds like something straight out of a bad horror novel, or a B-grade movie. But it's true." Sofia toyed with her mug, scratching at the side with a long fingernail, before moving to the handle. "My parents weren't excommunicated for their affair. They were expelled because Mama fell pregnant. They ended up in Galicia. We stayed for a while, but I didn't go to school until we moved to Rome and lived there for about a decade."

"Sounds like an exotic childhood." *Or a nightmare.*

"It was... *interesting*. Most kids don't have to deal with strangers popping into their house at all hours of the day and night because one of their kids *might* be possessed." Her smile was thin and didn't quite reach her eyes, but seemed sincere. "Papa got his accreditation as an exorcist from the Vatican before he was kicked out. And although the Church pulled their support, his faith in God never swayed. It gave him the strength and power to help those facing supernatural entities."

"So…" Kae wasn't sure how to broach the subject. How did you ask someone if they'd ever actually faced a demon? Or been present during an exorcism? "Uh, were you there when he, um… exorcised these kids?"

"I think I need more coffee." Sofia stood, grabbed her mug and filled it to the rim. "Do you want some?"

"No, I'm fine."

"Are you sure? You look like you could use an energy boost, and I'm all out of adrenaline. Or cocaine."

"What?"

"I'm joking. You really need to lighten up." Sofia headed back to the table with the coffee pot in hand. She poured more for Kae and sat across from her.

"Sorry, *I'm* all out of cheer at the moment."

"I understand," she said with a sigh. "And if things were as dire as you said before you left the house, they will only get worse."

She took a sip of her coffee because she didn't need any sort of expert to tell her this.

Kae didn't want to be rude, but wondered what the lingering taste in her coffee was. It wasn't entirely unpleasant, but made the liquid more bitter than usual.

"I know it's hard to deal with things that aren't easily explained by science, and let's be honest, reality." Sofia placed a hand over Kae's and it was warm, comforting. "You're questioning yourself, wondering if you're losing your mind. But whatever you saw is really happening. Unless you accept it, no one can help you. Not even me."

"That's the thing," she said, wiping the tears away with her free hand. "I do believe it. It's why I'm here." Kae sighed. "If Tessa hadn't mentioned you had an interest in this kind of stuff, I probably wouldn't have known where to turn."

"Well, I'm glad you came." She squeezed her hand and her eyes were bright. "I know you don't like me because you think I destroyed your marriage, but I'm not the one who betrayed you."

"That's not—"

"Don't lie to yourself, or to me. You'll always think of me as the woman who came between you and your husband." Sofia didn't remove her hand. "And I'll never be able to overcome the past, but I hope we can build a future. I love your kids as if they were my own, and since I can't have any…"

"Sorry. I didn't know." The truth was, she'd never given this woman a chance but she couldn't soften completely. "Look, I know you love our kids and you're good to them, but can you please refrain from filling Tessa's brain with all of this weird stuff? She's having more nightmares than usual." Kae had to say it. "I realize this makes me sound like a hypocrite when I'm here because—"

"It's fine, I get it."

She nodded but didn't add anything else.

"My life was never easy and I suffered the consequences of such bizarre knowledge. Before moving to America, I spent a year in a psychiatric ward in England. So, I understand why you don't want Tessa to be bombarded, and I haven't. I've kept things simple and haven't delved too deep. I mostly tell her about folklore and fairy tales. There'll be plenty of time for more serious subjects when she's older."

"Oh, I'm sorry to hear that." This woman always appeared to be so confident that she never would've guessed she'd spent even a minute in a psychiatric ward.

"I appreciate that." Sofia polished off her mug and sighed. "Both of my parents died during the first exorcism they let me watch. I begged them for months to take me along, told them I was ready. They finally agreed, but didn't let me participate…" Her voice trailed off and a sheen of sadness washed over her face. "The entity was strong and as soon as she noticed me, there was no stopping her. Mama and Papa died that night trying to protect me from the wrath of a demon. They died because I told them I was ready."

"Oh my God, that's awful!"

Sofia winced. "I was the only survivor and that's why I was hospitalized."

"I'm so sorry. About everything." She hadn't expected her snap decision to drive over to see Sofia to turn into a recounting of her very sad family history. Or that she'd find herself apologizing for Sofia's misfortunes so many times. At least she now knew two things—that Sofia could indeed help, and that she wouldn't be reckless with Tessa.

"It's okay, don't feel sad for me. The experience made me stronger and I was exonerated of all charges, because how can a looney bin like me have done something so heinous?"

As much as she was convinced coming here was the right move, she still felt bad for dredging up so many painful memories for Sofia. "Maybe it wasn't the best idea to come to you with all of this, I—"

"Don't be silly. I'm glad you came," she said with an earnest smile. "I have a wealth of information at my fingertips."

"Tessa told me."

"She's curious and reminds me of myself at that age." Sofia sighed and put the mug back on the table. "And that's why I won't be careless with her. I promise."

"Thank you," Kae said, and meant it. "Do you think we're dealing with a demon?"

"Probably."

"And it's been living inside my house? Inside my daughter?"

Sofia took a deep breath. "Kaelyn, your daughter's body is probably a haven for a horde of demons. After she came back, she might never have been there at all."

"But she went to the hospital and they constantly checked her, kept telling me about her vitals and all that other medical stuff."

"Okay…" She looked thoughtful. "They might have laid dormant, then."

"What does that mean?"

"When the demonic enter a human vessel, the soul is stripped away instantly but these entities need time to settle into the body, to incubate."

"Are you saying she was attacked by demons in the woods and then possessed?"

"Probably…"

"But why did it take sixteen months for her to come back?" None of this made any sense. "Why send her back at all?"

"Well, they inhabit the body until they're strong and can find other hosts. And according to what you said about her time in the hospital, when Molly came back, she was probably still alive. But once she left…"

"Are you saying my daughter's dead?" Her mind filled with Molly's physical deterioration, how she didn't speak, and that disgusting smell.

"I'm afraid so."

"Is the corpse of my daughter all that's left of her?"

"I'm terribly sorry, but the only answer to that is yes."

Kae's chest constricted and her breath caught inside her chest.

"I know this is hard to deal with, but you have to relax. We'll work through this together," she said in a soft and soothing voice. "Give me a second." She stood, disappeared down the stairs leading to the cellar and returned with a book in hand. "You know about Czort, right?"

Kae struggled to catch her breath. "The urban myth? Of course, that's been passed down for generations in Thicket, but it's not supposed to be real."

"Czort is the offspring of very powerful and violent Slavic gods." She dumped the book on the table in front of Kae and opened to a marked page.

"Why would a Slavic anything be living in our woods?"

"Gods, goddesses and demons aren't restricted in their geography. Just because they were birthed by one mythology, doesn't mean they can't exist elsewhere." Her eyes sparkled with knowledge. "Have you noticed how most gods have counterparts in many cultures around the world?"

She nodded, unable to tear her gaze away from the tiny letters in the book and the illustration of a huge shadowy humanoid creature. Horns, or antlers, made of branches stuck out from multiple places on his head, and even though the drawing was in black and white, she knew those eyes were aflame.

"It's because they can go anywhere, manifest wherever they see fit. The fact Czort hides in the woods surrounding Thicket shouldn't be a surprise. Czort spends most of his days and nights hibernating and survives on the chaos around him. He rarely leaves the confines of the woods but commands the shadows like tentacles."

"What?" She glanced at her sweater and although Sofia caught her, the other woman didn't say anything. Kae couldn't stop thinking about the black tendrils that held her son captive in the sunroom, or the tentacles that attacked her in Roy's backyard.

"Sometimes, he fertilizes demonic charges, and they're the ones who venture into the world in search of suitable vessels." She met her gaze, as if daring her to understand the underlining meaning. "Czort would be happy to keep these minions with him forever, but they get antsy."

"What do these—" Her voice broke because her mouth was dry. "What do they want?"

She shrugged. "A chance to wear a human body so they can cause chaos. It's what the demonic do. Some are just more calculating about their goals and actually use their intelligence. These particular minions are like mindless fools with only one thing on their collective mind—possession."

"And Molly is a vessel?"

"Yes."

The idea of her child's body being hollowed out to fit a multitude of demons made her gag. "But why her?"

"She probably caught his eye and when he tested her strength…"

"So, these demons entered Molly's body and are biding their time?" Kae swallowed the lump in her throat. "But what does Czort want?"

"He wants to get rid of the demons. If they're not going to enjoy the silence and the tranquil obscurity while absorbing the chaos, he wants to sever their ties." Sofia ran a long-nailed index finger down the page, stopped halfway. "When Czort finds a sturdy vessel able to survive the demonic onslaught, he takes the soul and his tentacled shadows prepare the body, fill it with the demons who want to leave. Then, he sends the shell back to the land of the living and lets them play."

She thought of those small fingertips trying to climb out of Molly's eyes and all the monstrous faces inside.

This is true, it's all *true.*

"Think I'm going to be sick." Kae ran out of the kitchen and stumbled into the bathroom, where she threw up only liquid. Her body vibrated wildly, so she rode the quivers until she started to feel the world right itself again.

Not that anything will ever be okay.

Kae stayed still until she felt stable enough to get off her knees. She flushed the toilet, cleaned her hands three times and rinsed her mouth out. All while ignoring the mirror because she didn't want to see how disheveled she was.

She couldn't believe Molly was a playground for the demonic. How could she get over such a revelation? Even if this all stayed between them, how could she live the rest of her life knowing such madness was real? And that she couldn't tell anyone else without the risk of being committed?

"Are you feeling better?" Sofia asked when she wandered back into the kitchen.

"Not really."

"I made you some chamomile tea, and you're going to have to eat at least two of these." She placed a plate of dry crackers in front of her. "Before you protest, you need to get some strength back. You look like you're about to pass out."

Kae cleared her achy throat and collapsed onto the chair. "Can we get Molly back?"

"I'm afraid not." Sofia drew in a breath and exhaled. "Molly's gone."

Tears blurred the table, crackers and the cup. Deep down inside she'd known her daughter was gone days ago. Maybe since the day she'd returned. Molly used to be a bright and beautiful spark, now she was a pit of darkness.

How could life be so cruel, and make her lose Molly *twice?*

"I know this is hard," Sofia said, softly. "But you have to be strong. For Tessa… and Tommy."

Kae blinked away her unshed tears and sipped the warm tea, which had the same bitter aftertaste as the coffee. She nibbled on a cracker, small bites were all she could manage, the only way to keep the crumbs from rising up her throat.

"You know, I always thought demons wanted to take over the world and that's why they possessed people," she finally said.

"Ah, yes, a very popular misconception exploited by fiction." Sofia shook her head. "Most demons don't want to stay in a human body forever. Actually, they despise the threat of being earthbound for too long."

"How can we stop these *demons?*"

"We can bind them to the vessel."

A throbbing started in the back of her head. "I'm not sure what you mean… but you're talking about Molly, aren't you?"

She nodded. "We have to wipe out the vessel before the demons branch out."

"What about Czort?"

"We can't eliminate or contain him, but if we destroy the demons he'll peacefully return to the woods."

"But if he draws these kinds of creatures to—"

"He's a benevolent being—"

"Not according to that verse."

Sofia sighed. "It's true that he might take a weary traveler here and there, but he's not a threat. Not like these demons."

"Are you sure?" Was that what happened to Billy? Was Roy's son one of these weary *travelers* she'd mentioned? Had Czort decided to take Roy as well? The thought made her heart ache all over again.

"Kaelyn, if we trap these demons, Molly's loss won't be in vain." She sighed and met her gaze. "They've already taken her and plan to take more people. You don't want that, do you?"

"Of course not!"

"Then we need to bind the demons to a vessel."

"I wish you'd stop referring to Molly that way."

"You're right, and I'm sorry. But I need you to understand the reality of what's happening, and what we have to do." The determination in her eyes intensified. "Can I count on you to help? If you can't do this, I'll go back to your house and deal with it my—"

"I can't let you go alone." Not after everything Sofia had just told her about the risk of exorcisms and how much demons cost her. Besides, she was right about Molly. Her heart might ache through every moment of what they were about to do, but what other choice did they have?

"Are you sure?"

"Yes."

"All right, then." Sofia pointed at a passage in the open book. "Molly is currently a conduit for the demons and soon, they'll escape to possess others. But if we bind them to her shell—*her body*—they'll be stuck."

Kae read between the lines and felt nauseated.

You have to remember that Molly's gone. That body in the sunroom isn't your daughter.

"How do we do that?"

"Via hypnotic suggestion, and by reciting the entire verse."

Kae vaguely remembered Tessa mentioning this.

"There are two parts to the verse." She pointed at the page. "It's what Czort uses to draw souls in. If you listen and surrender, you're pretty much his. He takes the soul and the body is usually discarded. But, with demons involved, that's when they take the opportunity to enter the vessel."

"How do we use that against them?"

Sofia sat down in the chair next to hers and took her hands. "Kaelyn, this is where you come in."

"How?"

"For starters, you're Molly's mother. Plus, I can't self-hypnotize."

"I don't know what you're talking about."

"I need to recite the verse to you via hypnosis, but will replace the word *surrender* with *expel*."

"What? No!"

"It's the only way." She tightened the grip on her fingers. "She's your blood and you share a bond that death can't sever completely."

"I don't like the sound of this."

"It won't hurt you or her."

Kae pulled her hands away and stood, paced the kitchen. "I don't want to be hypnotized—"

"As soon as you bind the demons inside her, it'll be done. Will only take a minute, if that." Her eyes sparkled. "It's the only way."

"There has to be another—"

"There isn't." Sofia sighed. "Well, we can ignore what we know and let the demons take their course..."

"What would happen then?"

She shrugged. "They'll probably possess most of Thicket."

Kae couldn't believe what she was hearing, refused to accept these terrible choices. Either give herself over to hypnosis performed by her ex-husband's wife, or let the town become a playground for supernatural beings.

The cellphone sitting on the kitchen table rang.

"I better get that," Sofia said. "It's Devin."

"Yeah, go ahead." She thought about the devastating situation she found herself in. How could she take part in destroying her daughter's body? And give herself over to suggestion so the task could be performed? But if she didn't, then others would be at risk. Too many people had already disappeared...

That girl inside your house isn't Molly.

Sofia's brow furrowed. "Yeah, Dev, she's right here." She handed her the phone. "He wants to talk to you."

"Hello?"

"What're you doing at my house?"

"I... wait a sec, where are you?" She heard her son saying something in the background. "And why aren't the kids at school?"

"We decided to take the day off," he said. "Why are you with Sofia?"

"It doesn't matter. What do you want?" She was losing patience with this man.

"I'm at your place. We wanted to surprise you and Molly, see if you guys wanted to get an ice cream with me and Tommy."

"Isn't Tessa with you?"

"She's with"—the line crackled—"we've been knocking on the door for ages—"

"Don't go into the house!"

"Why? Is it because you don't want me to see Molly—"

"No, it's because—"

"Dad, Molly's at the door."

"Wait a sec, Tommy."

"Whatever you do, don't go in the house," she practically screamed.

"I'm not going to leave now that Molly's answered the door." Devin's frustrated sigh echoed down the line. "Hi honey, how are you today? You don't look so good."

"Devin, please, get the kids and go. Now!"

The call dropped out, or he disconnected.

"Devin!" She glared at the phone displaying a wallpaper of Sofia and Devin. "Here, I have to go!"

"What's going on?"

"They're at the house and Molly answered the door."

Sofia's eyes widened as she stood. "We better get over there."

"You don't have to—"

"Yes, I do. Now, come on."

Kae wasn't sure what they would find, but she was starting to think the hypnosis option might be the only way to keep her kids safe.

1:00pm

Kae slammed on the brakes, almost smashing into the garage door but didn't care. She'd come close to hitting Emilia's blue car, which was still parked on the street. Where was the poor woman? Had she become another plaything for these damned demons?

She was about to rush out of the car but paused, turned to face the passenger seat. "Sofia, what's involved in this hypnosis thing?"

"I can do it right here, right now. It'll only take a minute."

"Yeah, but what will you do?"

"I've already told you. I'll recite both verses via hypnosis, but will replace the word *surrender* with *expel*."

"That's it?"

"Then, you have to look into Molly's eyes and recite the verses before she beats you to it."

"And you're sure I'll remember?"

"Positive."

Kae hated to do this, but nodded. "Okay, let's do it."

"Are you absolutely sure you can?"

"No, but let's do it anyway."

Sofia's lips curved into a smile. "You have no idea what a sacrifice you're making," she said. "Because of you, many lives will be spared."

She wanted to ask about the ones that had already been lost, but bit her tongue because every time she thought about Roy, the pain was too raw.

"What do I need to do?"

"Look into my eyes."

Kae kept her eyes glued to Sofia's green stare. Although she could see the woman's mouth enunciating, she didn't hear a single word. But she could feel her own lips responding.

Her mind was full of Sofia's smooth and melodic voice, so soft all she wanted to do was give into anything this woman said. She was putty in her hands.

Sofia clicked her fingers and Kae startled, blinked several times because her eyelids were stuck together.

"Um…" was all she could say.

"Now, you're ready," Sofia said. "Let's go."

"Are you… sure?" Nothing felt different. Well, except for a heavy sensation behind her eyes, like an ocular headache.

"Kaelyn, let's go!"

Her limbs were suddenly in action even though her brain was still trying to catch up. And before she realized what was happening, she'd run in through the open front door and was headed for the sunroom.

Focus on what you're doing.

This sounded different than her usual inner voice, but she listened anyway and took a couple of shallow breaths. The room stunk worse than the night before, smelled like something had died in here. And someone had… Molly.

She refused to let the same thing happen to the twins.

"Tessa, Tommy!"

"You're right about the smell," Sofia said beside her.

"Teresa! Thomas!"

Sofia grabbed her arm, stopped her from heading into the corridor. "Maybe we shouldn't give away that we're here."

"Too late for that." Kae looked around at all the mugs and glasses littering every surface. Some with dripping coffee stains, others with what she could only assume was blood and pus.

She was so horrified she didn't bother to cover her nose.

They're probably outside.

The thought came out of nowhere and she turned to find the backdoor was open.

"Mom!"

"That's my son." Her heart rattled inside her chest but she ran outside.

A tight grip on both of her shoulders made her jolt back to the reality she was slipping away from.

"Relax, it's me," Sofia whispered near her right ear.

She shivered at the proximity and wondered if this was a side effect of the hypnosis.

"Kaelyn, go to her."

"Go to who?"

"To Molly, of course"

"But she's not…" Yet, even as the words tumbled out, she spotted her eldest standing at the end of the yard. Silent tears slid down her face because she wasn't sure she could do this. "Molly?"

"I'm here, Mother." That wasn't her voice—*voices*—because there was definitely more than one coming from her.

"I can't do this."

"You can, and you will." Sofia's grip on her shoulders was too hard, her fingernails bit past her sweater and into her skin. "Go on. Open yourself to the truth."

Kae's legs took her closer, and she wasn't sure if she was commanding the movement or if someone else was. As she approached the tree line, the terrifying scene came into focus and she nearly collapsed.

"No."

Molly gripped Tommy's hand on her left and Devin's on her right. Tendrils of black smoke entered their eye sockets and open mouths, bits of ash floated around father and son. Behind the trio stood many familiar faces—neighbors, colleagues, people who lived on this street. And there was Emilia, the unfortunate counselor assigned to this doomed case, and Dr. Misra. Mew and Sienna. Even the deputy, Betty.

Too many ill-fated people who'd gotten caught up in this disastrous web.

But she couldn't find Roy, or Tessa.

"Where's Tessa?" Kae searched frantically, but she wasn't among the crowd being held captive by tentacles of smoke.

"Why don't you come closer, Mother?"

"Where is my daughter?"

"Kaelyn, listen to me." Sofia's nails dug deep into flesh. "Don't get distracted, or forget what you have to do. Go to her, *now!*"

"I have to find Tessa—"

"Concentrate!" Sofia's fingers were daggers inside her shoulders, piercing and filling her with the focus she needed. "I'll be right beside you."

"Okay…" There was only one thing left to do.

"Don't be afraid," Sofia whispered.

Every ounce of worry and concern slid from her mind and her heartbreak dissolved, replaced with a cool determination and confidence.

I can do this.

I will *do this.*

Kae fortified her thoughts and rushed toward the entities wearing Molly's body for their own perverse enjoyment.

With every step, more ash fell from the sky but she didn't care that it caught in her hair and eyelashes.

She stopped a few feet away.

Molly's unnerving smile was so wide the cracks on the sides of her mouth bled. Tiny ebony and yellow drops slid down her chin. She resembled a grotesque ventriloquist dummy.

"Hi, *Mother.*"

"You're not my daughter."

"Sure, I am. Come here and I'll show you that I am." Molly released her brother and father, extended both of her pale and bloody hands. Soot stained the skin that wasn't cracked and bleeding.

"Now's your chance," Sofia whispered.

"There's someone here who wants to see you."

The same monster Kae thought she'd spotted behind Roy's house was suddenly there. All his proportions were wrong because the longer she stared, the more she realized this was a man.

A man whose body had been bent and twisted beyond recognition.

The pitiful creature opened his mouth and grunted, used his crooked hands and feet to scurry along the underbrush like a contortionist forever stuck in a hellish backbend.

"Don't you recognize him?"

She did, but this couldn't be... *Roy.*

"Mother, take my hand and I'll sing the pretty verse for you." *"Now!"*

Was that Sofia?

A sharp pain struck between her eyes, blinded her for a second. When the world returned, she found herself standing in front of Molly and they were holding hands.

"Will you join us?"

Kae's mouth started the chant instantly before Molly could.

"If you venture into the woods alone, he'll be waiting for you. If you look deep into his eyes, he'll come for you. If you're brave enough to stay, he'll never let you go."

Molly's dark eyes were pinned on hers and she wasn't sure who was controlling who, but she continued. *"If you keep your eyes open, you'll see the darkness. If you stare into the void, you'll fall into the darkness. If you surrender your soul, I'll suffer the darkness."*

A multitude of tiny demons writhed inside those black pits.

"I command you, horde of demons who serve Czort, to leave the ailing vessel and enter this fresh one." Kae's ears heard the command but couldn't stop saying the terrible words. She was in the passenger seat and someone else was driving.

Tiny fingers popped out of Molly's eye sockets, crawled out so fast Kae didn't realize what was happening until the minions were climbing into *her* eyes and pushing their way into *her* mouth.

Her mind blacked out and when she jolted back into herself, she said, "I bind you to me for now and all eternity."

Molly lay on the grass like a deflated doll.

Kae wanted to crumple beside her, to cradle what was left of her daughter but she couldn't maneuver her limbs. Too many whispers were fighting for attention inside her skull.

Tommy, Devin and all the others were standing still with ashy tentacles keeping them in place like statues.

A mighty yell echoed from the woods and the ground shuddered. A pair of large, fiery eyes appeared above the trees.

2:00pm

The backyard was suddenly engulfed by darkness.

Even after shrinking from a giant into an eight-foot monster, this beastly creature with branched horns sprouting from his head was as majestic as he was terrifying. His body was obsidian and seemed to be made out of bark and leaves. Shadowed tendrils spread from his bulk, each one connected to a captured resident of Thicket.

Tessa was right, he's a tree man.

Those red eyes burned like flames as he tilted his head back and growled.

Kae raced back to the house, and when she reached the backdoor, was surprised to see Sofia was no longer with her.

"Sofia!"

"Get inside the house," she called from somewhere.

"What about you?"

"Just, go! They're coming."

"What?" She glanced over her shoulder and spotted all the tentacled people being dragged as Czort loomed over the house. Her vision blurred as she searched for her kids, but couldn't find them. Either way, she'd lost Molly *and* the twins.

She'd lost everyone she loved. How could she survive this torment?

Somehow, Kae drew the strength to run into the sunroom and slammed the door.

Czort smashed against the side of the house hard enough to shake the foundations. She barely made it out of the sunroom before a giant, clawed hand tore open the roof like a can of sardines. He'd grown in stature again. How did he regulate his size?

She continued into the kitchen, but his claws demolished that as well.

With half of the house missing, the others had crowded inside and were getting closer.

Kae turned to head for the front door but a sudden pain in her midsection made her double over. Unbearable pressure pressed against her eyelids and when she rubbed her eyes, was disgusted to find small fingers squirming against hers.

What's happening to me?

Small skittering shadows compromised her vision and tiny fingertips pulled on her internal organs.

The cloying smell of gas raced up her nose and made her cough. She stumbled into the corridor, hoping to escape this house of horrors.

Where was Sofia? Why had she disappeared, and what were those commands she'd uttered outside?

Everything was muddled and her mind was racing, but she couldn't deny the suspicion any longer. The one she didn't want to accept.

Kae moaned in pain as her guts quivered. She lifted her sweater with shaky fingers and found a small leg and a hand pushing against her flesh.

She cried out and gagged at the realization of what was inside her. What went wrong out there? Sofia told her Molly was the vessel and that they would bind these demons to her… but her daughter's body was nothing but discarded skin now.

Kae doubled over in agony.

Another fist pounded into the roof and some of the ceiling caved in, barely missing her head. She tripped over something blocking her way, and when she landed awkwardly on the other side, she found the twisted man she'd spotted outside. How did he get inside before she did?

You should know better than to ask impossible questions by now.

He skulked closer, over her. A piece of the ceiling struck his stomach because he'd shielded her with his bent body. How could he endure such torture and still be alive?

This was another horrible realization she could no longer ignore.

"Roy?" She crawled out from under his curved body and stared into his familiar, but now permanently upside-down eyes. "It *is* you!"

A guttural growl ripped through the opening at the end of the hallway, where Czort's fiery eyes spat embers that lit up the carpet.

"He's going to burn the house down!"

"Kae."

She ran her fingers through Roy's lush hair and couldn't stop the tears. "What did they do to you?"

"I…"

"I'm sorry you got involved in all of this." With his torso bent completely out of shape, the man she loved was more wounded animal than human. But she could see the emotion shining in his eyes. "I love you so much, I always did."

What did Sofia say about Czort? That he took weary travelers? Did he also destroy their bodies if they didn't surrender willingly? Was that what happened to Roy?

"You were always…" He gasped, struggled to form the words. "… love of my… life."

As Kae's tears slid down her face, she reached up and kissed his cold lips.

"You… should… go."

"I can't." The door was a few steps away but she wasn't going anywhere.

How could Kae tell him a horde of demons were shifting inside her? That if she didn't stay to the very end, all of these creatures would infect even more than the people who'd already lost their lives. Because the realization came too late. It was only now that she understood her mistake. How she'd put her trust in someone who'd ultimately betrayed her.

The hypnosis had turned Kae into the vessel, and now she had to burn with these demons and what was left of those who'd followed her into the house. She could already hear them shrieking, but it would get much worse.

Czort's sizzling eyes had started the fire, but the gas would blow this place to kingdom come in a matter of minutes.

Was that Sofia's plan from the beginning? But what did she want?

You know exactly who I want.

Sofia's voice haunted her because that response was definitely from her. Kae recalled her youngest mentioning how Other Mother was going to teach her all about the interesting folk and fairy tales she knew.

"Kae... please."

She touched Roy's face and regretted every wrong move she'd made during this horrible week. And when she spotted Czort towering over them, she welcomed the end.

His eyes were scorching fire-pits and as she watched, the flames spread along his antlers, chest and arms. Flowed down his torso and legs until he was a luminous fireball ready to consume everyone and everything within reach.

Kae pressed her forehead against his. "Roy, I—"

The explosion ate her words.

AFTER

Saturday
November 14, 2015

6:33am

It was chilly out but Sofia was sitting on the back porch drinking her third beer.

Kaelyn's house burned to the ground with everyone trapped inside its belly, and she'd stood in the shadows until the black smoke with horned antlers rolled back into the woods. It hadn't taken long for her to walk down the familiar streets until she'd reached the safety of her home to make sure Tessa was where she'd left her.

As expected, the preteen had been sound asleep and wouldn't wake up until later this morning. And when she did, Sofia would make sure every trace of her father, mother and siblings were wiped from her mind.

She couldn't help but snicker because Kaelyn hadn't noticed Tessa was here all along while she'd told her longwinded tale of woe. She hadn't even suspected Sofia of any wrongdoing, even though the woman resented her from the beginning. She did become concerned when Kae ran to the bathroom and then resisted the idea of hypnosis, but good old Devin had come through. And she hadn't even planned that little call.

Either way, Sofia knew from experience that if someone was pushed far enough, they eventually turned to *anyone* willing to help—even the woman who'd stolen her husband.

None of that mattered now. That pesky woman was as gone as the burden of a man she'd called her husband longer than she'd intended. The only thing she'd wanted was finally all hers.

And Tessa would never find out the truth.

At one stage, she'd thought Molly might be the one, but that teenager was too much like her mother. In the end, Molly had served an even better purpose.

Sofia stared at the tree line long enough for her eyes to blur. Then again, the blurring could be from the heady combination of success and beer.

A few seconds before the sun rose above the canopy of green, the glowing eyes appeared, lost in the tangle of branches and dense leaves.

"Welcome back," she said, tipping her bottle.

"As promised, the debt was paid."

"Everyone died? We didn't leave any loose ends?" She despised loose ends because they were messy, and traceable.

"No one survived." His raspy voice echoed inside her mind. *"Not even you."*

"Perfect." As far as the authorities were concerned, everyone wearing the name of Roscoe was now dead. "I expected nothing less from the son of gods and monsters."

He waited patiently.

"I release you."

Czort lowered his horned head in salute and melted into the woods to take a well-deserved hibernation. The horde of demoniacs had haunted him far too long, and their destruction was well overdue.

Of course, he wouldn't have been as obliging if she hadn't bound him to the task, or if he knew the reason all those pesky demons attached themselves to him was because *she'd* summoned them. But he didn't need to know the extent of her manipulation. All that mattered was that Czort was free of demons, and she finally had a ripe new shell for future use.

Sofia stretched and sighed, content for the first time in years.

Everything she'd told Kaelyn about her past was true, but she'd embellished a bit and failed to mention the events happened in the early part of the twentieth century.

Sofia's father was indeed an excommunicated Catholic priest ordained by the Vatican as an exorcist. Her mother, a respected nun in a well-known convent who spent most of her life dealing with stigmata and her own demons. Together, they'd fought the cliché of good versus evil and died for their cause.

Their strong and shared belief in God hadn't spared them in the end.

Father Adan and Sister Consuelo were devout to their religion until their deaths, but couldn't save their daughter. On the night they died while battling a greater demon, the couple were too weak to defeat the *Princess from Hell* who'd entered their beloved Sofia Torres-Urbina.

But their daughter did something neither of them could— survived. And she didn't need God to do it. Sure, there was nothing left of the sweet Sofia they'd raised together, but *she'd* fortified this lovely shell for decades.

The time to slip from this body and into a new one is near.

Sofia sipped on her favourite beverage while dreaming of a dark future.

Acknowledgments

I wrote the first draft of this story during a strange time, when life was changing and my role as a parent was turning into something completely different to what it used to be when our daughter was small. It's a change we all go through and while it's never easy and has plenty of hiccups, I found it easier than expected to enter into a new way of life… that was really what it used to be before we had a child.

During all of this, an idea struck me about a mother who loses her teenage daughter not because it's the natural way of things, but because she goes jogging one morning and doesn't come back. After that, she wishes her daughter would come home every single day but, when she eventually returns, things don't go as expected. While revising this story, it became something so much darker and more involved. I'm very proud of my love letter to small-town horror about a dysfunctional family forced to face supernatural evil.

I'd like to thank Andrew Robert and DarkLit Press for contracting this creepy tale of mine, and for his enthusiasm and expertise while fine-tuning all the behind-the-scenes stuff.

And of course, I want to thank my husband Eugene for his endless support and understanding about my need to tell these strange stories. As well as his pep talks during the darkest hours when I get lost in doubt and need him to pull me out. Also, Cassandra, for her part in helping shape my warped storyteller's mind into stranger directions. As well as her cheerleading.

Finally, thank YOU for reading this book.

A Note From DarkLit Press

All of us at DarkLit Press want to thank you for taking the time to read this book. Words cannot describe how grateful we are knowing that you spent your valuable time and hard-earned money on our publication. We appreciate any and all feedback from readers, good or bad. Reviews are extremely helpful for indie authors and small businesses (like us). We hope you'll take a moment to share your thoughts on Amazon, Goodreads and/or BookBub.

You can also find us on all the major social platforms including Facebook, Instagram, and Twitter. Our horror community newsletter comes jam-packed with giveaways, free or deeply discounted books, deals on apparel, writing opportunities, and insights from genre enthusiasts.

VISIT OUR LITTLE-FREE-LIBRARY OF HORRORS!

About the Author

Yolanda lives in Sydney, Australia with her awesome husband and cheeky cat.

Writing is something she's been doing since her teens, and never gets tired of it. She enjoys writing in a variety of genres, but all of her stories are shadowed by darkness because she can't keep the horror out of every tale.

When Yolanda's not writing, she likes to watch movies, her favourite TV shows, going for long walks, and reading. She's a HUGE reader. She loves books--both writing and reading them! She's a total bibliophile.

www.yolandasfetsos.com

Content Warnings

Violence

Death

Parental Trauma

Grief

Mental Illness

Child Endangerment

Supernatural Horror

Printed in Poland
by Amazon Fulfillment
Poland Sp. z o.o., Wrocław

22763240R00083